THE HAUNTED PAST

A LIN COFFIN COZY MYSTERY BOOK 11

J. A. WHITING

Copyright 2019 J.A. Whiting Books and Whitemark Publishing

Cover copyright 2019 Signifer Book Design

Formatting by Signifer Book Design

Proofreading by Donna Rich: donnarich@me.com

This book is a work of fiction. Names, characters, places, or incidents are products of the author's imagination or are used fictitiously. Any resemblance to locales, actual events, or persons, living or dead, is entirely coincidental.

All rights reserved.

No part of this publication can be reproduced or transmitted in any form or by any means, electronic or mechanical, without permission in writing from J. A. Whiting.

To hear about new books and book sales, please sign up for my mailing list at:
www.jawhiting.com

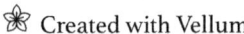 Created with Vellum

For my family with love

1

Although the April air was chilly, the sun was bright in the beautiful blue sky as the tourists and townsfolk crowded Main Street to watch the Daffodil Festival's antique car parade. More than one hundred vintage cars were decorated with daffodils, yellow and white streamers and ribbons, yellow balloons, and garlands of flowers. The huge urn in the center of the street was full to bursting with yellow flowers. The spectators joined in by wearing yellow clothes, scarves, and crazy hats festooned with daffodils, feathers, and any other yellow object someone could think to stick on a hat. One family wore bonnets with foot-tall lighthouses attached to the tops and decorated with flowers. Even the dogs wore yellow collars with daffodils on them.

The Daffodil Festival, a celebration of spring, went on for several days with most activities clustered on Friday, Saturday, and Sunday including a tailgate picnic in Siasconset, the Daffodil 5k race, the Daffodil Flower Show, scavenger hunts, free concerts on the beach, and an open-air marketplace selling food, clothing, crafts, jewelry, and artwork. The island was bursting with yellow, white, light orange, and pale pink daffodils blooming along the bike paths, in flower boxes, in gardens, pots, and at the sides of the roads.

Thirty-year-old Carolin "Lin" Coffin and her cousin, Viv, wore big brimmed hats. Lin co-owned a landscaping company on the island so her hat was decorated with flowers, miniature gardening tools, and yellow ribbon. Because Viv owned the bookstore café on Main Street, her hat was adorned with tiny books and plastic cakes and muffins with a yellow glittery garland wrapped all around. The young women's boyfriends, Jeff and John, wore yellow ties and vests, yellow socks, and yellow and white checkered caps.

Standing with the Coffin cousins to watch the parade were island historian, Anton Wilson, lifelong Nantucket resident, Libby Hartnett, and art gallery owners, the Snow family, Robert, Lila, and their nine-year-old grandson, Chase. The previous December, Lin, Robert, and Chase had been in a harrowing situation where their lives had been in danger, but they were saved by keeping their wits about them and working together to outwit the criminal who threatened them.

"Look, Lin." Chase pointed down the road. "It's an antique fire truck."

"Later today, they're giving kids a ride on the truck," Lin told the youngster.

"Can we go?" Chase eagerly asked his granddad. "Can I get a ride?"

With a smile, Robert put his arm around the boy's shoulders. "Sure you can. We'll walk over after lunch."

The gold highlights in Viv's chin-length, light brown hair glittered in the sunlight. A little shorter than her cousin, she and Lin were like sisters, and since Lin had moved back to Nantucket, the two young women had been instrumental in helping to solve several mysteries. Lin and Viv were descendants of the Coffin family, original island settlers, some of whom had unusual skills and abilities which had been passed down to the cousins.

Since returning to the place of her birth, Lin had been able to see ghosts, and during the investigation of one recent case, Viv had seen the spirit of her ancestor. Reluctant and uneasy about it, Viv hoped she would never see another ghost ever again.

Over the past year, Lin had become more accepting of her skill and she would never turn her back on a ghost who appeared to her for assistance.

When the parade was over, everyone piled into cars to head to the quaint village of Sconset for the picnic and on arrival, they found a spot on the green lawn overlooking the ocean and spread out their blankets and beach chairs. Salads, grilled chicken, baked potatoes with different toppings, veggie tacos, shoestring fries, fruit salad, and baked beans were set up buffet style at the back of Lin's truck.

A yellow and white checkered cloth had been spread over the bed of the truck and pots of flowers were placed in between the serving platters. Bottles of wine, seltzer, and a pitcher of lemonade were lined up next to the glasses and napkins. With grumbling stomachs, the friends took plates and filled them with the delicious food choices.

"How are the wedding plans coming along?" Lila Snow asked Lin and Viv.

The Haunted Past

The cousins and their future husbands became engaged on the same evening and had decided to have a double wedding in September at the boat club overlooking the water.

"We have the band booked." Lin's blue eyes brightened as she smiled at Viv. Viv and John had been in a band together for years and their bandmates offered to play for the upcoming wedding.

"We picked out the appetizers and the meals, too," Viv said.

"A friend is going to do the flowers for us," Lin told Lila. "And Viv wants to make the cakes, but I think it will be too much work. She should relax and enjoy the time instead of fussing with the cakes."

"Lin has a point," Lila said.

Viv gave a shrug. "I'll be stressed out anyway so I may as well do the baking and decorating. It will keep me busy and take my mind off things."

John and Jeff walked over.

"I told her not to do it," John said, "but I may as well be spitting in the wind. When Viv gets an idea in her head, that's it."

Jeff said with a grin, "I'm keeping out of it."

Lila asked, "What are your dresses like?"

Lin and Viv exchanged quick looks.

"We haven't picked them out yet," Lin admitted.

"What?" Lila's eyes went wide. "The wedding is only five months away. You two better get on with it."

After the main meal was finished and desserts were brought out, Robert Snow approached Lin.

"I have a favor to ask you." Tall and slender, in his mid-sixties, with white hair and blue eyes, Robert, and his wife had lived in a large, three-story Colonial in town for over thirty years and had experienced the presence of a ghost in their house. For them and their family, sharing the house with the ghost of Captain Samuel Baker was a normal part of their lives, although they didn't share that information with just anyone.

A flicker of nervousness slipped over Lin's skin and she brushed her long, brunette hair back from her face. "What can I help with?"

"I have a friend who recently moved to the island," Robert said. "He's actually the son of my friend. The young man's name is Tim Pierce. He inherited a house on Old Lane at the top of Main Street."

When Robert paused, Lin asked, "Is everything okay?"

"Some things came with the house. It's an antique Colonial that was built in the early 1700s,"

Robert said. "The house was owned by my friend's father and when he passed away, the place was left to the family. My friend is settled in Boston, but his son was eager to move here so he inherited the house. Some of the original furniture came with it."

"That's great. Your friend's son is lucky to have those things."

Robert nodded. "Tim's father is aware that the island is known to have a lot of ... *activity*."

Lin knew Robert was referring to ghostly activity.

"Tim doesn't quite believe such things are possible," Robert added.

Lin's eyes narrowed. "Is something going on in the house?"

"It seems so." Robert took in a breath. "It seems there's a table."

Lin cocked her head waiting to hear what Robert was about to share.

"The table jiggles."

"Jiggles?" Lin couldn't help but smile. "Maybe Tim needs to stick a bit of paper under one of the legs to even it out so it doesn't wobble."

"That would be an easy fix." Robert shook his head slightly.

"Is there more to the table than jiggling?" Lin asked.

Robert made eye contact with Lin. "It seems so. Would you come and have a look at it?"

"Me? Why?"

"I think the piece of furniture ... well, I think there's something going on that could use your attention."

"What kind of a table is this?" Lin asked.

"It's a three-legged, tilt-table. It's made of walnut. The top is about thirty-one inches across. It's quite a lovely piece. We think it's been passed down with the house each time it's been sold," Robert explained. "There are a few scuff marks on it, but that's to be expected."

"What do you want me to do?" Lin asked.

"Could you come take a look at it?" Robert asked. "Tim doesn't want to keep the table, but my friend doesn't want him to sell it since it's been in the family for ages and he doesn't think it's right to part with it."

"Does your friend want it?"

"No. He thinks it should stay on the island."

Lin was feeling more and more anxious. "Does your friend want it to stay in the house?"

"Not necessarily."

Lin gave Robert a look of apprehension. "You want me to take it?"

"Could you come have a look and see what you think? Lila and I would consider taking it, but you know how Captain Baker can be. We think it might upset our ghost if we bring the table home."

"Is there a ghost in the table?" Lin asked with a tone of skepticism.

Robert kept his voice down. "We don't think there's a ghost *in* the table. We think there's a ghost that might be associated with the table."

"Has this table always been jiggling?"

"Occasionally, I guess. Not often. It seems to happen mostly around the Daffodil Festival. But it seems to be becoming more active for some reason. We thought you might be able to figure it out."

When Lin agreed to take a look at the table, she and Robert decided to meet at Tim Pierce's home the next day. Robert thanked Lin and went to get another drink from the truck.

Viv walked over carrying two plates each with a slice of cake on them. She handed one to her cousin. "What's wrong with you?" Viv's eyes darkened suspiciously. "I know that look."

Lin accepted the plate with the delicious-looking dessert. "We have something to do tomorrow afternoon."

"What's that?" Viv's voice held a tone of wariness. "What are you dragging me into this time?"

"We're going to have a look at an antique table."

"Oh, okay." Viv visibly relaxed ... until she heard her cousin's next sentence.

Lin added, "A haunted table."

2

The antique Colonial was yellow with a dark red door and a flower garden set behind a white picket fence. Mature trees stood tall around the periphery of the property, their leaves still small and light green, but ready to fully leaf-out in a matter of a week or two.

"Early 1700s?" Viv stood next to her cousin, both of them gazing at the fine old house.

Lin nodded. "That's what Robert said."

Viv nervously pushed a strand of her hair behind her ear. "You don't think this table will jump around when we're looking at it, do you?"

"I don't know what to expect," Lin admitted.

"If I suddenly have to leave, you know where to

find me." Viv looked over her shoulder plotting her escape.

"Don't run away," Lin chided. "I need you to stay with me. I'd like to hear your opinion once we see the table."

Robert hurried along the brick sidewalk towards them and he waved when he spotted the cousins near the house. "Hello. I'm a few minutes late," he apologized. "Someone was looking at a painting in the gallery and I didn't want to push them into making a decision."

"We only just got here ourselves," Lin said. "It's a beautiful house."

"My friend's father was meticulous about keeping the Colonial in tip-top condition." Robert walked with the young women to the front door where he rang the bell setting off a melodious chiming that could be heard coming from inside the foyer.

The door opened almost immediately and Tim Pierce greeted his guests with a smile. "Come in. Nice to see you, Robert."

Lin and Viv were introduced and the young man asked if they'd like a tour.

Thirty-two-years old, Tim was tall with broad shoulders and a slim build that hinted at him being a runner. He had dark brown hair and blue eyes, a handsome, friendly face and a sunny disposition.

"This is the sitting room. The dining room is on the other side of the foyer near the parlor." Tim showed them the rooms decorated with period antiques, rugs in muted colors, and carefully chosen accessories. "There's a wood-paneled library with loads of built-in bookshelves and a fireplace." Tim led them down the hall to the room he'd just described, and then he took the guests to see the kitchen.

The space had tall ceilings, white cabinets, high-end appliances, a long island, and granite countertops, with a beautiful wood floor completing the chef's kitchen. Large windows looked out to the lawn and gardens and allowed natural light to flood the room.

Tim showed them another sitting room and a glass conservatory, each looking like something out of an architectural magazine.

"What a gorgeous place," Viv gushed.

"I'm lucky to have inherited the house. My family and I spent a lot of time in this home with my grandparents when I was little, and I can't believe my good fortune to now be its owner." Tim had them sit down on the comfortable white sofas in the conservatory where pitchers of water and lemonade had been set out along with a carafe of coffee and a platter of cookies.

"When did you move in?" Lin sipped from her glass of lemonade.

"About three weeks ago." Tim passed around the plate of cookies. "The home was fully-furnished so all I had to do was bring my suitcases."

"What do you do for work?" Viv asked. "Do you have to go back to the mainland often?"

"I own an architectural firm with offices in Boston and Hyannis. I can do most of my work from here, but I will have to travel to the offices for meetings. Most of my time will be spent on-island though." Tim had a wide grin on his face. "I love it here. I've loved it since I was a little child. I always imagined making a permanent home on the island, but I never dreamed I'd own my grandfather's house."

After more conversation, Lin brought up the reason they'd come. "We hear you have a piece of furniture that you might not want to keep."

Tim's face lost its cheery expression. "That's right. It's an antique table. I don't really know what to do with it," he said uncomfortably.

"Can you tell us why it makes you feel that way?" Lin asked with an encouraging tone of voice.

"I don't know how to explain it." Tim looked over at Robert Snow, and the older man gave a nod.

"We've had our own share of unusual objects," Lin explained.

"I'll say." Viv sighed and rolled her eyes.

"We've also heard and seen some unusual things," Lin told the man. "You can speak freely with us."

Tim shifted a little on the sofa, clearly feeling uneasy and a little tense.

"It's your grandfather's table, is that right?" Robert tried to get the discussion started.

"It is." Tim looked almost embarrassed to talk about it. "It's called a tea table. It's one of those tilt tables with an oval top. The piece is made of walnut. It's a beautiful piece of furniture."

"Was it here in the house when you visited as a child?" Lin asked.

Tim nodded. "It's always been here."

"You don't want to keep it?"

Tim let out a breath of air. "Maybe not. Maybe it should go somewhere else for a while and then come back one day. I need a break."

Viv's eyebrows shot up her forehead. "Why do you need a break from it?"

Tim lifted his hands in a helpless gesture. "It jiggles. It drives me nuts."

"Can you tell us a little about what happens?" Lin questioned.

"The table used to be in the front sitting room. Its legs start to shake sometimes ... it jiggles, sort of moves a bit from side to side, but fast." Tim shrugged. "It's almost like the table is in a house that's experiencing an earthquake."

"How often does it happen?" Lin asked.

"Lately, it's been happening a lot. Four or five times during the day. About three times during the night. It wakes me up. It's pretty noisy."

"Do you recall this happening when you used to visit?"

"I never saw it behave this way when we visited my grandfather, but my dad told me about it a couple of times," Tim said. "Dad told me the table sometimes wiggled and bumped around and that everyone ignored it whenever it had an *episode*. I don't believe in paranormal-type things. I think there has to be an earthly, scientific explanation for unusual activity," the young man told them. "This has me baffled though. I put pads under the legs, I moved it to different spots in the rooms, I put a rug under it. I thought it might have to do with atmospheric pressure changes, but it doesn't seem to matter what kind of weather we're having. It jiggles on warm days, cold days, rainy days, sunny days. Nothing matters. It still jiggles and pounds against the floor. I can't figure it out." Tim sighed and then said quietly, "Things seem to be escalating. It's jiggling more often. I don't know what to do with it. I've given up ... for now."

"You moved it out of the sitting room?" Lin questioned.

"I put it in the small room I use as a laundry room. I put a pad under it so I don't have to hear the banging and bumping." Tim shook his head again.

When Lin asked if they could see it, Viv's face seemed to pale.

"Of course." Tim stood and led the guests to the laundry room off the kitchen.

It was a bigger space than Lin thought it would be with a washer and dryer, a granite counter for folding clothes, a pole between two walls for hanging clothes, and cabinetry for storing cleaning and washing supplies.

The walnut table stood at the far end of the room, it's tabletop tilted to the side.

As soon as Lin had stepped into the room, she'd felt so cold inside that she almost shivered. Moving across the room, she stood in front of the table without speaking.

Tim, Viv, and Robert watched from their spot near the door.

One of the legs began to shake as if a heavy man was walking across the floor, the vibrations of his feet causing the slightest of movement.

Lin watched.

The shaking became more insistent. The jiggling of the legs making a bump-bump-bump-bump noise against the tile floor.

Not wanting to speak aloud, she thought the words in her head.

I'm here. I want to help you, if there's something you need.

Lin rested her hand on the table, and as soon as she touched the wood, a flash of icy cold ran through her veins ... and the table stopped its shuddering.

"How did you do that?" Tim hurried over to Lin. "How did you get it to stop?"

"I put my hand on it." Lin's eyes ran over the details of the piece, all the while thinking about the many people over the past hundreds of years who had seen and touched the tilt table.

"Were the legs uneven on the floor?" Tim glanced under the antique piece of furniture.

"I don't think so." Lin's body was wrapped in a current of icy air and she took a look around the room to find the ghostly source, but no one showed themselves. Whenever a spirit materialized nearby, the freezing air would swoop around her until the ghost disappeared.

Tim turned to Lin. "Do you think it will happen again?"

She answered with a quiet voice. "I think so."

With a sigh, Tim's blue eyes met Lin's. "Can you take it for a while? Maybe you can figure out what the problem is."

Lin rested her hand on the table again. "I can try."

3

Viv eyed the table in the corner of Lin's kitchen. "Are you going to keep it there?"

"I thought I would. Then I can keep an eye on it." Lin was working on a home-made vegetable pizza for her and Viv's dinner.

Nicky, Lin's small mixed breed brown dog, was resting on a dog bed near the screened door with Viv's gray cat, Queenie.

"Wouldn't it be better in your office?" Viv spoke warily. "Maybe it would like to be by itself."

Lin chuckled. "A little bumping and hopping won't hurt us."

Viv stood at the kitchen island making a salad to go with the pizza. "At least it's been quiet since we got it home. Maybe it likes it here. Maybe it will stay still here."

Spreading the chopped veggies over the top of the pizza, Lin asked, "What did you think of Tim Pierce?"

"He's a lucky duck inheriting that huge Colonial house. He seems nice. He's cute, and he's similar to me ... the fewer ghosts and odd happenings in our lives, the more we like it."

"Do you think he really believes that there's some earthly explanation for what the table has been doing?" Lin took a quick glance at the piece in the corner.

"I think he's hoping so." Viv gently mixed some blueberries into the green salad. "What do you think is going on?"

"I don't know. According to Tim and Robert, the table has jiggled like this in the past, a few times a year, often around daffodil time, but not as violently as Tim claims it's been doing. And he told us it's been happening regularly since he moved in."

"Could the table be missing Tim's grandfather?" Viv asked. "It's been a short time since the man passed away."

Lin looked up. "That sounds like a possibility except for one thing."

"What's that?" Viv raised an eyebrow.

"The table is an inanimate object. There has to be a ghost connected to it somehow for it to be able to move."

"How?" Viv asked.

"How what?"

"How can a ghost be connected to a piece of furniture?"

"I mean a ghost has to be making the table move. The ghost isn't *in* the table."

"What do you think it wants?" Viv glanced around the room with an uncomfortable look on her face.

"I guess this is our latest mystery to solve." Lin sprinkled some grated Parmesan cheese over the top of the pizza.

Viv grunted. "Maybe this time, at least, there won't be any danger of us getting killed while we solve it. But I wouldn't bet on it," she muttered. "Have you called Libby?"

Lin nodded. "She's going to try and come over in a couple of hours. She wants to see the table."

"Maybe she'll want to take it home with her," Viv said hopefully. "She might need more time to look it over."

"It's staying here. If I'm going to help this ghost, I need to have the table close by."

Viv carried the finished salad to the table. "Can you sense what he wants? I'm assuming it's a *he*."

"I get cold when I'm near the table, but I don't have any idea what might be needed by the ghost." Lin slipped the pizza into the oven and set the timer. "And why now? Why was the table fairly quiet all those years while Tim's grandfather had it?"

The cousins took glasses of wine out to the deck and the dog and cat padded outside with them.

Lin's grandfather had raised her after her parents died when she little, and she inherited her cottage from him. The house was built in the shape of a horseshoe with the kitchen-dining room at one leg of the shoe, the living room in the center, and her bedroom and a small bedroom she used as an office on the other leg of the horseshoe. There was an unfinished second floor that she and Jeff planned to build out over time once they were married and he moved in with her. A large deck had been built inside the three parts of the horseshoe and it overlooked the trees and brush of the fields behind the house beyond the stone patios.

"So the timing of the jiggling table must be a clue." Viv was stretched out on a lounge chair sipping her wine. "Why is it causing a ruckus now? What's going on that has the ghost upset?"

Lin was quiet as she watched Nicky and Queenie walking around in the field. "I'm going to need more information if we're going to figure this out."

"I'm sure there will be a ghostly visitation very soon." Viv didn't look happy about the possibility. "Do you know anything about Tim's grandfather?"

"Very little. Robert told me the grandfather moved to Nantucket when he was in his early fifties and bought the Colonial. He owned a couple of stores in town. I think the table tapping has its connections further back in time rather than with Tim's grandfather."

"But why is the ghost upset now?" Viv asked. "What's set it off? What's going on?"

When the pizza was done, Viv and Lin ate outside at the picnic table and sat around talking as the sun set and the sky darkened. The air turned chilly and they were heading back inside the house when the doorbell rang.

Anton Wilson, carrying a plate of chocolate chip cookies, and Libby Hartnett went into the kitchen to see the tilt-top table.

Libby, an older woman with pretty silver-white hair and blue eyes, had lived on Nantucket all of her life, growing up on her family's farm in the middle of the island. A descendant of the Witchard family and a distant cousin of Lin's and Viv's, she had paranormal skills of her own and had spent a good amount of time helping Lin understand the world of unusual abilities.

"Where is the piece?" Libby spotted the item in the corner. "Has it been quiet since you brought it home?"

"Nothing has happened," Lin told them as she made tea for everyone. "It's been a normal table."

Libby gently ran her hand over the wood. "It's old. Mid-1700s. It could tell us a lot of stories."

Anton stood back slightly looking a little bit wary of the object. "It hasn't done anything since it's been here?"

"Nothing," Viv said.

They took their tea and the cookies into the living room where Lin had lit the gas fireplace and they settled on the sofas. Nicky and Queenie rested on the rug by the cozy fire.

"Libby has been telling me about table tipping." Anton took a cookie from the plate.

"What's that?" Viv had never heard about the phenomenon.

Libby held her teacup in her hand. "It started in

the 1700s. There was a movement where communicating with spirits became popular. There was a rise in professional mediums, psychics, and spiritualists. Table tipping or table turning came into fashion. Some believed it was a way to communicate with spirits, others enjoyed it as a fun parlor game. A group of people would sit around a table with the lights dimmed. They would ask questions and the table would lift slightly and provide answers either by tapping a certain way for *yes* and a different way for *no*. Another method of use was to ask a question and allow the table to tap any number of times to spell out a word. For instance, two taps would mean the letter *B*. Someone would sit with a pad and pencil and write down the letters that the table spelled out."

Viv blinked. "It sounds sort of like a séance."

"Similar, yes." Libby nodded.

"Do you think *this* table is trying to communicate that way?" Lin's heart pounded.

"We could try it and see," Libby offered.

"Oh." Viv sat up straight. "Is it safe to do this?"

"It's perfectly safe, my dear," Libby said.

"Libby thinks a ghost may be trying to send a message by using the table to tap out letters," Anton said. "It sounds ridiculous to me, but I suppose any paranormal activity could be pooh-poohed by people. Why not try it and see what happens?"

"What do we have to do?" Viv's voice was shaky.

Libby said, "We sit together at the table and place our hands on the top, palms down. We ask a question and wait to see if we receive a response. If tapping begins, the note-taker will count the taps and write down the corresponding letter. This continues until the message is completed."

"Can I be the note-taker?" Viv asked. "I don't want to sit at the table."

"That's fine. Shall we?" Libby asked matter-of-factly.

The tilt-top table was set up in the middle of the kitchen and Lin and Viv brought three chairs out from the office and the bedroom and placed them around the table.

Viv took a seat at the island with the pad and pencil on the counter.

Anton and Lin sat down, Libby dimmed the lights, and took the third seat, and they placed the palms of their hands on the table.

After sitting in silence for a minute, Libby spoke. "We wait for the spirit to communicate with us."

Two minutes passed and nothing happened.

Libby tried again. "We are open to receiving your message."

They waited for five minutes and still nothing happened.

Lin's heart was racing when she spoke. "How can we help you? What do you need? Who are you?"

Another five minutes passed without incident.

Libby started to speak. "It seems...."

A cold whoosh of air enveloped Lin ... and then the table lifted a half-inch off the floor and began to vibrate.

Lin's and Anton's eyes went wide with shock and Viv held the pencil in the air as she stared in horror at the piece of furniture. Nicky and Queenie sat up and watched with keen eyes.

"Keep your hands on the table," Libby urged with a whisper. "Don't take them off."

The table shuddered and tipped a little from side to side. Its legs went down and touched the floor, then it lifted an inch and hovered there for a few seconds before hitting the floor like it had been dropped. Up it went, down it slammed. Over and over until it began touching the floor, one leg of the table at a time.

Tap. Tap. Tap. Tap. Tap.

Viv stared without moving.

"Vivian," Libby said firmly. "Count the taps. There were five of them. The corresponding letter is E."

Viv shook herself. She grabbed the pencil and wrote down the letter, then listened as the table began another sequence of tapping, and then continued eight more times.

When it was finished, the table rose two inches into the air and came down with a loud boom.

No one spoke for a few seconds until Viv said, "I think I'm going to faint."

"Before you do," Libby said, "what is the message you wrote down?"

Viv looked at the paper like she was seeing it for the first time. "It's not really a message. It's a name." She looked over at the people sitting around the table. "The table spelled out ... Ezra Cooper."

Viv began to sway in her seat and Lin rushed to her side before her cousin could topple onto the floor.

Holding Viv in her arms, Lin looked down at the letters written on the pad of paper.

Ezra Cooper.

That's my ghost. Now what does he need?

4

Lin and Leonard Reed, her landscaping partner, stood at the back of his truck unloading hydrangea bushes and gardening tools. Leonard, in his sixties, had brown hair with a bit of gray mixed in and dark brown eyes. The man was tall with muscular arms and shoulders from years of doing landscaping work.

"And then the table lifted off the floor and tapped one of its legs a number of times to correspond with a letter of the alphabet." Lin's arms were covered with soil from carrying the bushes out of the truck.

Leonard frowned and stared at his partner. "Are you kidding me?"

"I'm not. I swear, it's the truth. The table has been

jiggling and tapping in Tim Pierce's house since he moved in. Libby got the idea to try the table tipping. Nicky was there. He saw what happened."

Nicky, sitting on the lawn watching the two people work, let out a yip.

"Table tipping is a load of bunk, Coffin. People used to do it for entertainment."

"I know. Libby told us people enjoyed it as a parlor game, and most of the time, it was just idle amusement." Lin made eye contact with Leonard. "But, sometimes, it isn't."

"I don't believe it." Leonard hauled a wheelbarrow from the truck bed.

"The tapping spelled out a name. Ezra Cooper. We heard the taps. Viv counted them. The associated letters spelled it out. Tomorrow we're going to the historical museum to do some research on the man."

"I bet you won't find anything."

"Viv didn't make up the name," Lin protested.

"You all got excited by the possibility that the table is inhabited by a ghost."

Lin put a hand on her hip. "The table isn't inhabited by a ghost. A ghost is using it to communicate with us. I saw it tap when we were at Tim's house.

Everyone else saw it, too. Why would we all make it up?"

Leonard made a grunting noise. "I still say its bunk."

Just then a blue convertible pulled over and stopped beside them.

Heather Jenness, a woman Leonard had been dating, was at the wheel and a young woman who looked to be in her mid-twenties sat in the passenger seat. In her fifties, Heather was attractive with shoulder-length, light brown hair and pretty eyes. She owned a law firm on the island and had met Leonard at a fundraiser for the Shipwreck Museum. At first, Leonard balked at the idea of dating, but with Lin's encouragement, he and Heather had been enjoying each other's company over the last few months.

"I saw your truck." Heather gave Leonard a warm smile and said hello to Lin. "This is my niece, Lori Michaels. She's staying here through the summer to work in my office. I hope she'll stay even longer."

"Nice to meet you." Lori had big blue eyes, sandy-colored hair that fell just below her shoulders, and a friendly smile.

"Lori's an attorney," Heather said. "I need

another associate so I invited her to come for a few months and try out living on an island."

"I've always wanted to live on Nantucket," Lori told Lin and Leonard. "I love everything about the island."

"I was born here," Lin told the young woman. "I lived off-island for a few years and then moved back last year. It was the best decision I ever made."

Heather looked to Leonard. "Are we still on for dinner at my house tomorrow?"

The man smiled and gave a nod. "I'll be there. I'll bring some craft beer and I'm making a cake."

"Wonderful. You're the best baker." Heather gave a him a big smile.

"I've told him a million times he made the wrong career choice," Lin teased. "He should have been a pastry chef."

"I'll see you tomorrow evening," Leonard told his new girlfriend.

Waving their hands goodbye, Heather and her niece drove away down the street.

"Things are going well I see." Lin looked at her partner out of the corner of her eye.

"Mm-hmm." Leonard heaved one of the bushes into the wheelbarrow.

"What does that noise mean? It's going great? It's

okay? I like her?"

"I'm not discussing my dating life."

"Oh, for Pete's sake, if not for me, you'd be sitting at home feeling sorry for yourself every night," Lin grumped. "I deserve updates every now and then."

Leonard was silent as he pushed the wheelbarrow to the rear yard with Lin jogging after him carrying some tools. "Oh, no, you don't. You aren't allowed to ignore my questions."

Nicky trotted along behind wagging his tiny tail.

"You mean I'm not allowed to ignore your nagging."

"Call it what you will." Lin put the shovel on the grass near the new bed of flowering bushes they were creating for the homeowner. "You have to give me *something* ... I care about you. I need to know how things are going."

Leonard set the bush down and stretched his back. "I like her. She's nice. I enjoy her company."

Lin's face was triumphant as she pumped her fist in the air. "I knew it."

"You did not." Leonard pushed the wheelbarrow back to the truck.

"Yes, I did. I knew she was right for you." A wide grin spread over Lin's face. "I knew you'd have fun together."

"Now you're a psychic?" Leonard glanced over his shoulder. "I thought you could only see ghosts."

"I have many talents." Lin lifted another hydrangea into the barrow.

"Yeah, I know." Leonard used the back of his hand to wipe at some perspiration on his forehead. "Nagging being one of them."

Nicky plopped on the grass in the shade and while Lin and Leonard dug the holes in the new border, the conversation shifted back to the antique table.

"So do you think the table was bumping around because there's a spirit trapped in it?" Leonard was still skeptical.

"There isn't a ghost trapped in it. A ghost is using it to send a message." Lin leaned on the shovel.

"What's the message?"

"The name. Ezra Cooper."

"Is that the ghost's name or is it a name that means something to him?"

Lin stopped working for a second. "I don't know. My initial thought was that the name was the ghost's, but maybe that's wrong. Maybe the name doesn't belong to the spirit. Maybe he wants me to investigate something about a man named Ezra Cooper."

"Keep an open mind."

Lin tamped soil around the newly-planted bush. "So you no longer think the table tipping was bunk?"

"I didn't say that, but at least, you got a name from your parlor game," Leonard told her. "See where it all leads. You might want to try the game again. The ghost might give you more than just a name ... he might decide to give you the reason for his communication."

"I've never been that lucky." Lin sighed. "Viv always asks why the spirits don't come right out and tell me what they want. Why do they only hint at things?"

"She's got a point."

"She sure does. Maybe one day, I'll be able to communicate with ghosts mentally. On the last case we worked on, I received a message from Sebastian without him verbalizing it. I heard it in my mind. Maybe that ability will expand one day."

Sebastian Coffin was an early settler of Nantucket and Lin was one of his descendants. He and his wife, Emily, sometimes appeared to Lin in their spirit forms to warn her of something or to hint at what she needed to look for when helping a ghost.

"Maybe you and I will learn to communicate like

that. I'll send you a sentence that I'm thinking about and you'll receive it in your head," Leonard said.

"That would be cool," Lin smiled.

"What's Tim Pierce like?" Lifting the next plant, Leonard eased it into one of the freshly-dug holes.

"He's in his early thirties, personable, bright. He seems nice. He owns an architectural firm so he'll have to travel to Hyannis and Boston once in a while for meetings."

"He inherited the Colonial house?"

Lin told her partner that Tim inherited the house from his grandfather. "Tim's dad didn't want the house so Tim was the lucky recipient."

"How far back do his ancestors go on the island?" Leonard asked.

"Just to the grandfather I think. Tim's family wasn't one of the early settlers of Nantucket. The grandfather moved here and purchased the house. He didn't inherit it from anyone." Lin cocked her head. "Why do you ask?"

Leonard gave a shrug. "I was wondering if Tim is related to the ghost who's sending you messages through a table."

"He couldn't be, could he?"

"It all depends on where the ghost is from. If he's from the island, then he's probably not related to

The Haunted Past

Tim since he's only the second member of his family to own the Colonial house. If the ghost is from elsewhere, I guess it's possible for him and Tim to be related somehow."

Lin's forehead creased in thought. "We'll have to find out who the ghost is, who Ezra Cooper is, and whether or not Tim or Ezra has a connection to the house. My guess is that one of them has some sort of tie to the house."

"Why is there suddenly *activity* around the house?" Leonard questioned. "What's happened to set the ghost off?"

"Robert Snow told me that there's always been some activity with the antique table around the time the daffodils bloom, but that it's been some minor jiggling and shaking. This year was different."

"Is it because the grandfather passed away and now there's a new owner?"

"The grandfather's will stipulated that either his son or his grandson could inherit the house."

"But maybe this ghost, whoever he is, isn't happy about Tim being the owner."

"That could be." Lin lifted the shovel. "I guess I have some digging to do."

"That's right, Coffin." Leonard chuckled. "Both here in the garden, *and* in the library."

5

It was late afternoon when Lin and Viv entered the stately historical museum and headed for the library section at the back of the building. The museum's librarian, Felix Harper, greeted Lin and Viv.

"Planning on doing some research today?" Felix, an expert on Nantucket history, was tall and thin, with salt and pepper hair and blue eyes. The man took fashion seriously and was always dressed in stylish, tailored clothes. He wore gray slacks, a crisp black and white striped shirt, and a fitted black suit jacket.

"We're trying to find some information on a man named Ezra Cooper. He lived on-island in the 1700s," Lin told the librarian. "We don't have any other details about him."

"Follow me and I'll set you up on the computers. I'll roll over a fiche machine in case you need older records than what's been uploaded online." Felix led the way to the long tables with a bank of computers lined up on one of them.

The cousins settled in for what they expected to be a long session of searching for any material that mentioned Ezra Cooper.

"Where should we start?" Viv asked. "We don't have a specific date. We're only guessing the ghost is from the 1700s."

"Let's do a search on the man's name and include the word, Nantucket." Lin's fingers flew over the keyboard, and they waited for the search results to display. When Lin clicked on one of the entries, her face lit up. "Look. Here's something."

"An obituary?" Viv was shocked to see results so quickly in their search. "What does it say?"

Lin summarized. "The date of the entry is May 27, 1781. Ezra Cooper, a mason, passed away last week at the age of twenty-eight. His wife, Abigail, died the year before at the age of twenty-four on April 25. That's all that's written." Lin sat straight. "April 25. That's daffodil time."

Viv's face showed understanding. "That must be why the table shakes around the time of the Daffodil

Festival. Does the entry state the causes of the couple's deaths?"

Lin glanced back to the screen. "No. Just the names, dates, and ages. That's it."

"Is there a way to find out more?" Viv asked.

"We can ask Felix," Lin suggested.

Felix bustled over and took a look at what Lin had found. He leaned against the table and began to type. "There are some ledgers that have been put online recently. We might find a bit more detail." In a few seconds, Felix said, "Here we are. Let's see."

Lin tried to look over his shoulder.

"Abigail Cooper died as a result of a fall," Felix said.

Viv asked, "A fall? What kind of a fall?"

"It doesn't say."

"What about Ezra?" Lin asked.

Felix sighed. "Suicide."

"What?" Lin's voice expressed shock.

"I translated what's written here," Felix told them. "It's says self-imposed which implies the man died by his own hand."

"Gosh." Viv's hand went to her neck.

"Ezra died a year after Abigail passed away," Lin noted in a soft tone. "He must have been in a state of grief. He probably didn't want to live without her."

"How terrible," Viv whispered.

"Is there an address listed?" Lin asked.

"No, but we can search land records." Felix tapped away in a manner that made Lin think of the table tipping episode.

"Ezra purchased a house on Old Lane in 1777." Felix read the description of the place.

"Okay. Good," Lin said. "That's the house we thought he lived in."

Felix had to return to the front room to help another patron so Lin and Viv searched through records to find the date Ezra and Abigail were married. It took them an hour, but finally they found what they were looking for.

"They were married on May 1, 1778," Viv said. "Abigail died two years later."

Lin shook her head. "And then Ezra passed away a year after his wife."

"Is Ezra your ghost?" Viv asked in a soft voice checking that no one was standing nearby.

"I think so."

"I can understand why the ghost makes the table shake around the time the daffodils are in bloom," Viv said. "But what's different this year? Why is the ghost so insistent? Why is he making the table rattle so much?"

"I don't think the table will shake anymore." Lin's eyes narrowed in thought. "At least, not as much. I think the ghost was trying to get a point across."

"What's the point he's trying to make?" Viv asked carefully, not sure she really wanted to hear the answer.

"I think he wants someone to know who he was. I think he wants someone to know what happened to them."

"Why now though?" Viv asked.

"We have more digging to do," Lin said.

∼

Lin and Viv took the chance that Tim Pierce would be at home. When they knocked, it took a few minutes, but when the man opened the door, he looked surprised to see them on his front steps.

"Is everything okay?" Tim asked.

"Yes. We've been doing some research on your house and the prior occupants," Lin said. "Do you have a few minutes to talk? We can come back another time if you're in the middle of something."

"Come in. I just finished up for the day." Tim stepped back so they could enter. "I'm never really finished for the day. I'll work a few hours more later in the evening." The young man led the way to the conservatory.

Lin explained what they'd found in the historical museum library.

"He killed himself?" Tim's eyes were wide. "It's so sad."

"Do you have any information about some of the early owners of your house?" Viv asked the man.

"I don't have anything. I can ask my father if he has anything. Maybe he heard some things from my grandfather about the house."

"That would be really helpful," Lin said.

Tim shifted around in his chair and his voice was tentative when he asked, "Do these people's deaths have something to do with the antique table?"

"It's possible."

Tim exhaled and looked at Lin. "Robert told me you can see ghosts."

Lin's heart began to race. "Did he?"

"Robert and Lila believe there's a ghost living in their house," Tim said.

Lin nodded. Several months ago, she'd had interactions with the Snows' ghost.

"I have a hard time with this stuff," Tim said. "Maybe it's because I studied science and math, and things in the abstract throw me for a loop."

Lin smiled. "Math and science require abstract thinking. Being an architect, you need spatial-relation thinking skills. You need to think in the abstract to see a design in your mind."

Tim rubbed at his face. "Maybe *abstract* isn't the right word."

"There are things that exist in space and time, even if we can't comprehend them," Lin explained.

"You've really seen ghosts?"

Lin gave an almost imperceptible nod of her head.

"Wow." Tim leaned forward and clasped his hands between his legs. "I want to ask questions, but I don't even know how to start."

Viv smiled. "Welcome to my life."

Tim looked at Viv. "You two are related. Can you see ghosts, too?"

Viv swallowed. "Only once. That was enough for me. Ghosts are Lin's territory, not mine."

"Does my table shake because of Ezra and Abigail Cooper?" Tim asked warily.

"Maybe. We aren't certain yet," Lin said.

"Did they own the table?"

Lin held her hands up in a gesture of helplessness. "Maybe?"

"There must be something going on right now that caused the table to act up. Is that right?"

"That's what we're thinking," Viv said.

"Would it be okay if I walked around the house for a few minutes?" Lin asked.

Tim's eyes went wide. "Sure. Of course."

"You and Viv can walk with me," Lin said.

The three of them got up and Lin started moving through the house with Viv and Tim following behind her. As she moved down the hall, into the kitchen, dining room, and sitting rooms, she tried to pick up on anything a ghost might be trying to tell her. She waited for an icy chill to surround her, but it never happened.

"I'm not sensing anything," Lin said disappointedly.

"What happens when you see spirits?" Tim asked with genuine interest. "Why do they show themselves to you?"

"They need something. They need me to help them with something. And when I manage to help, they end up crossing over."

Tim sucked in a long breath and shook his head. "I can't believe I'm having this conversation."

Lin nodded. "It's not an easy thing to talk about, even for me."

Viv explained, "Lin doesn't have a choice. The ghosts show up even though she'd rather just be normal."

Lin gave her cousin the eye. "I *am* normal."

Viv ignored the comment. "They show up because Lin can help them. When they need her, she can't *not* help them."

"All of this sort of blows my mind," Tim told the young women. "But I can tell you're both good people. If there's something *I* can do to help, well, just tell me what to do."

Walking to the front door, Lin asked, "Are you settling in to your new home?"

"Yeah, I am. I love this house. I feel more at home here than I've ever felt anywhere else."

Lin and Viv said goodnight to Tim and headed down the front walkway to the dark street.

"I guess our visit didn't help much," Viv said with a sigh.

"Well at least, Tim is opening up to the idea of spirits."

When they reached the sidewalk, Lin suddenly stopped walking, and when Viv noticed, she spun around. "What's wrong?"

A wave of icy air surrounded Lin and she

glanced across the cobblestoned street to the opposite sidewalk.

A man wearing 18th century clothes stood staring at her. The atoms of his body shimmered and he appeared almost see-through. He made eye contact with Lin, gave a slight nod, and then his form flared and his atoms spun wildly until they sparked and disappeared.

"Lin." Viv rushed to her cousin's side.

Lin blinked at the empty spot on the sidewalk. "Our visit here *was* helpful. I just met Ezra Cooper."

6

Lin, Jeff, Viv, and John walked into town for the evening team scavenger hunt and they joined a crowd of people gathering in front of the historical museum for the instructions and list of questions.

John went to the registration table to sign up their team and he came back with questions in a sealed envelope and stickers for them to wear indicating they were taking part in the game. When everyone was ready, the organizers would ring a bell and then the teams would open the envelopes and begin the hunt. There was a time limit of one hour to complete the task.

"I'm excited," Viv rubbed her hands together. "We almost won last year. We only got one question wrong."

Lin nodded. "And we have to be quick. The team who answers the most questions correctly and gets back here the fastest will be the winner."

"Everyone put their game faces on," Jeff advised. "It's almost time for the bell."

John held the envelope ready to rip it open.

Viv laughed. "We're not competitive in the least, are we?"

The bell rang and John pulled out the questions and handed a sheet of paper to each of his team members.

"Let's read through all of them first, then we can decide on a route so we can get done as quickly as possible." John read aloud. "First question, find the addresses of the three historic Nantucket mansions called 'The Three Bricks.'"

"Easy one," Jeff said. "The instructions say we have to use our phone to take a photo of the team in front of every place described in the questions."

Lin, Jeff, and Viv attempted to group the questions geographically to make their search as fast as possible, and when they were ready, the foursome darted up Main Street.

When they'd written down the addresses of the Three Bricks, they had to find the house that was depicted on the questionnaire and answer several questions about it.

They tore through the town neighborhoods, finding the places, writing down the answers, and taking their photo in front of the stops they made.

"I think that's it," Viv said. "Let's go."

The team jogged back to town and raced to the historical museum.

"Are we the first team to return?" John wondered out loud.

The woman and man working at the table, checked the time and wrote it at the top of the scavenger hunt questions and then passed the paper to the judges to score and arrange according to the percentage correct and the return-times.

In thirty minutes, the winners would be announced and the prizes awarded so to pass the time, Lin, Jeff, John, and Viv strolled down to the docks to see the boats.

"I think we did well," Viv told the others. "I think we got all the questions right. We'll just have to see if our time was good enough for a prize."

A chilly breeze blew off the water as darkness descended over the island.

Lin told the men what had happened the

previous evening outside of Tim Pierce's house and they both began asking questions.

"What does this ghost want?" John asked. "Is Ezra Cooper the ghost telling you things through the table or is he someone the ghost used to know?"

"My feeling is that Ezra is the one speaking to us through the table," Lin shared what she thought.

Jeff asked, "Do you have any idea what he wants?"

"Not yet. His wife, Abigail, died from injuries sustained in a fall and Ezra took his own life a year later," Lin explained.

Viv shook her head sadly. "It seems Ezra couldn't go on after he lost his wife."

"How did Abigail fall? Do you know anything about the accident? Where it happened? What the circumstances were?" Jeff took Lin's hand in his as they walked along the docks.

"We don't know anything about her fall and I think that information is important to figuring out what Ezra wants me to do," Lin said.

"How can you find out what happened to the woman?" John questioned.

"We checked records at the historical museum library, but there wasn't a whole lot about the couple," Viv shared. "We're meeting with Anton tomorrow to see if there's anywhere else we can look for more details."

"The Coopers owned Tim Pierce's house?" John asked.

"Ezra lived there for four years. He bought the house in 1777 and he and Abigail married in 1778. Abigail died two years later, and Ezra passed away a year after his wife."

"They were cheated out of their future together," Jeff said wistfully.

"How old were they when they died?" John questioned.

Viv said, "Abigail was twenty-four and Ezra was twenty-eight."

"Heck, we're all already older than they were. They certainly were cheated," John shook his head.

Checking the time, Viv said, "We'd better get back for the results of the scavenger hunt."

The president of the historical museum stood on the top steps of the building with a crowd spread out in front of her as she announced the winners. First prize went to a five-person team who completed the questions with 100 percent correct and a time of 39 minutes. The second and third place teams were announced next.

"Finally, our fourth place team with 100 percent

correct and a time of 49 minutes goes to Lin and Viv Coffin, Jeff Whitney, and John Clayton."

A whoop went up from the four of them and John hurried up the steps to accept the prize.

"What did we win?" Viv was almost jumping up and down with excitement watching John open the envelope.

A broad smile crossed John's face. "It's a gift card to our favorite restaurant."

"Want to use it now?" Jeff asked. "We haven't had dinner yet."

The couples headed to the pub located next to the harbor and were seated by the windows where they could look out at the lights glittering over the dark water.

"I didn't think there was a fourth prize. I thought the historical museum only gave out first, second, and third place awards." Viv raised her glass of craft beer. "To a scavenger hunt well-played."

Everyone clinked their glasses.

"Wait until next year," John told them with a grin. "We'll win that first place award yet."

"It was a lot of fun, and I had the very best teammates," Lin smiled. "Those are the most important things."

"You're right, Lin," John admitted. Then he

narrowed his eyes and added in a jokingly serious tone, "But, next year ... must win ... the first place prize."

When the meals arrived and everyone was enjoying what they'd ordered, Lin said, "I forgot to tell you. Tim Pierce hired Leonard and I to handle his yard. He'll have to travel to the mainland pretty often and he's very busy. The yard is huge, but it's in a state of neglect. Tim's grandfather didn't keep it up in his last few years. Leonard and I are drawing up some landscaping plans." Lin smiled. "When we're done, it's going to be beautiful."

"What do you have planned for the space?" Jeff asked.

"New flowerbeds, lots of heirloom plants, a border of hydrangeas, a water feature, and a large two-tiered patio off the conservatory."

"Sounds great," John remarked.

"Leonard and I will meet with Tim soon to go over the plans. I'm excited about working on it. That house is a beauty, it needs a gorgeous lawn and gardens to go with it."

"How does Tim feel about having a ghost living in the house with him?" John asked. "It would freak me out." John was uncomfortable with the idea of spirits remaining on the earth and when Lin and Viv revealed to him their ability to see ghosts, he took the news much better than anyone expected. They talked long into the night about things none of them really understood, and John accepted the Coffin cousins' skills even though he was wary, nervous, and unsure about ghosts moving through the world.

Viv said, "Tim doesn't really believe in ghosts, but he seems to be opening his mind to the possibility that something is going on that can't be explained within earthly parameters. He's thoughtful and not closed-minded at all."

"I bet he's glad to have that table out of his house." John shook some pepper over his chicken.

"I don't think the table is going to be so *insistent* anymore," Lin said. "I think Ezra used it to send a message and he might not need the table's help any longer. I asked Tim if he was ready to take it back, but he wants to wait a little longer."

John shook his head. "I'd want to wait forever. I couldn't live in a house with ghosts. If I were the Snows, I would have moved out of their place a long time ago."

"The Snows like their ghost," Lin said. "They've never seen the captain, but they know when he's around and they're happy he's part of their lives."

John took a long swallow of his beer. "Just please,

don't tell me if there's ever one around me. I'd faint dead away."

While the others chatted, Lin's mind wandered to Ezra Cooper and his too brief life. Just when things were beginning for him and his wife, it was all cut short. How terrible for him to lose his young wife. Ezra must have fallen into a deep despair that he couldn't climb out of. *What does he want me to discover? There's so little to go on. How will I ever figure it out?*

Lin's heart was heavy and she was feeling a little hopeless when Jeff leaned close to her, looked into her eyes, and ran his fingers over her cheek in such a sweet and loving way that it lifted her spirits and made her so grateful to have him in her life.

I won't give up, Ezra. I'll figure out what you need.

7
———

Lin and Viv sat with Anton at the long wooden table in the man's antique Cape Cod house. The evening was cool and Anton had made a fire in the big kitchen fireplace and Nicky was asleep on the rug in front of it. Books and notebooks and two laptops sat on the table near the historian. Tea and coffee and a plate of cornbread and cookies were on the counter for the cousins to help themselves.

"Did you find anything?" Lin asked with a tinge of excitement in her tone.

"I found plenty ... whether anything pertains to your case is yet to be seen." Anton flipped through a history book.

"Did you read anything about Abigail?" Viv asked.

Anton looked over the top of his glass frames at the young women. "In a minute, I'll go over everything with you."

Lin and Viv sipped their tea trying to wait patiently for Anton to collect his notes.

"Yes, here we are." Anton finally spoke. "Ezra Cooper was a mason and bricklayer. I believe he had some other masons working for him. He was born on-island. His father was a merchant in town who appears to have done very well. It was the custom back then for people of means to help out their children by providing some assistance when they were starting out, so I assume the father gave Ezra some money to help him purchase the Colonial on Old Lane. All of this was pieced together through my historical knowledge of the island and by my sleuthing. Nothing is definitive, mind you, but I'm relatively confidant about it."

"You found quite a bit of information," Lin praised the historian.

"What about Abigail?" Viv questioned eagerly. "Were you able to find anything about her?"

"Unmarried women often did work outside of the home, but because they usually weren't allowed to keep their wages, there are very few records available about specific women of the time." Anton shuffled some papers around. "Women who worked taught school, worked as assistants in stores or apothecaries, did sewing or other domestic chores. Some women did own businesses and worked as blacksmiths, barbers, printers, tavern keepers, and merchants."

"What about Abigail?" Viv asked again.

"We know that Abigail's father owned an apothecary in town. The man's wife passed away when Abigail was probably a teen. I expect that she worked alongside her father until she was married, and even then, she may have worked in her father's shop a few days a week. Once children came along, most women stayed at home to care for them and take care of the household."

"Was Abigail born on Nantucket?" Lin asked.

"Oh, yes, I forgot to mention that. Yes, she was born on-island."

"Did you find any mention of the fall that took her life?" Lin questioned.

"There is a brief mention of Abigail Cooper experiencing an accident in town one evening in April 1780. The short article mentions a fall, but gives no details about where it happened or what her injuries were," Anton told them. "So it wasn't of much help. That's all I was able to find, just a few small things you didn't know."

"It's good information." Lin thanked the historian. "It's more than what we knew. So Abigail's fall must have been an accident and not the result of foul play?"

"If it had been foul play, there would have been something in the story about that. It seems the woman fell somehow and the fall resulted in her death. Most likely, she hit her head. It was an unexpected and unusual occurrence, a freak accident."

"Ezra must have been devastated," Viv said softly. "They must have had plans for a family, things they hoped for the future. All gone in a matter of seconds." She looked to her cousin. "If there was no foul play involved in Abigail's death, what could your ghost want from you? There isn't a murder to solve."

"I've been wondering the same thing," Lin admitted.

Viv's eyes widened. "Unless Ezra *didn't* take his own life. Maybe he was murdered. He might want you to investigate what happened to *him*."

Lin's head started to spin. "Do we know how Ezra died?"

Anton's face screwed up and he started to search

through his notebooks. "I don't recall reading anything about the man's cause of death."

"How could we ever investigate Ezra's death?" Lin asked with a look of worry on her face. "There are so few records available and back then, it was probably frowned on to reveal a suicide so we won't know for sure how he died. Even if we read everything written from the time and Ezra *was* murdered, we'll never be able to find out who killed him. There's nothing to go on. I doubt very much that we'll find a diary where someone confesses to killing Ezra. It just can't be done."

"Where are Ezra and Abigail buried?" Viv wanted to know.

Anton clicked on his laptop. "They're both buried in Old North Cemetery on Grove Lane."

"That's what? A quarter of a mile from Tim Pierce's house? So close to where Ezra and Abigail lived." Lin leaned over Anton's shoulder. "Can you locate the graves using the town cemetery website?"

"Let me take a look." Anton scrolled through the site. "Here it is. See?" He pointed to the screen.

Lin took note of where the graves were located in the cemetery. "I have an idea."

Viv gave her cousin a look. "Why do I know I won't like it?"

"Does anyone want to take a drive over to the cemetery?"

"I knew it. I knew I wouldn't like it," Viv sighed.

"Now?" Anton pushed his glasses up to the bridge of his nose. "Can't you go in the daylight? The cemetery's probably closed."

"It's never closed," Lin said. "Maybe the town doesn't want anyone to go poking around in there at night, but it doesn't close."

"What do you want to do in there?" Anton asked suspiciously.

Lin shrugged. "I just want to walk around, visit the graves."

"Why don't we do it tomorrow?" Viv suggested.

"I'd really like to go now."

Viv stood with a resigned expression on her face and looked at Anton. "Come on. I know better than to argue with her. We aren't going to win this fight. Let's get it over with."

Nicky sprang to his feet wagging his tail.

Viv saw the dog's reaction. "I'm glad someone's happy about this visit."

"It's not such an awful thing to do," Lin told them with a shake of her head.

"Walking around in the dark at night in a deserted cemetery?" Viv asked. "I think you and I hold two very different definitions of the word *awful*."

~

Lin parked her truck at the entrance to the cemetery and she and her passengers got out. Viv and Anton flicked on flashlights and they started into the graveyard with the dog sniffing the ground ahead of them. The moon was nearly full and it shined its silvery light over the landscape. Off in the distance, the spring peeper frogs' chirping calls sounded like a chorus of tiny sleigh bells and an owl hooted low and deep from somewhere in the woods.

"If it wasn't so creepy being in here, it would actually be pretty." Viv moved the beam of her light over the grass.

"It is pretty," Lin agreed with that part of her cousin's sentence.

"I'm pretty sure we're not supposed to be in here." Anton had looked around for a sign reporting the cemetery hours, but he didn't see one.

"We won't be long." Lin remembered where the Coopers' graves were located on the online map and she tried to apply that to the actual topography of the place. "I think it's this way."

As they walked, Anton used his flashlight to see the grave markers and when he swept the beam to the next row, the light found Nicky sitting near a grave, tapping his tail.

"I think Nick found it," Lin said hurrying over to see.

"How could the dog find it before we did?" Anton questioned.

"Don't even ask," Viv told him.

"Here it is. Here's the headstone. Here are their graves." Lin bent at the waist to read the nearly worn-away inscription, and saw Ezra's and Abigail's names on the stone. The dates were difficult to make out from the letters and numbers being so weathered and faded away. Lin gently touched the marker. "So very long ago."

The wind blew through the trees making the not-yet-mature leaves rustle in the breeze. Unsure of exactly why she'd wanted to come to the cemetery, Lin closed her eyes and bowed her head slightly trying to focus on the things that floated on the air. She knew that emotions and feelings could linger ... some for a very long time.

Lin began to feel dizzy and she had the weird sensation that her feet weren't touching the ground, like she was suspended a few inches over the earth, light as a feather.

Images flashed in her head ... two people sitting by a fire, a couple holding hands, a man's hand running tenderly over a woman's long hair. The pictures she saw in her mind never showed the couple's faces, they were always in shadow or seen from the back, but Lin knew who they were and the love they shared with one another touched her heart.

The peeper frogs' chorus of chirps sounded mournful to Lin's ears and the wind whipped suddenly around her and lifted her hair from her shoulders. The peaceful night turned lonely and forlorn and Lin shuddered from the weight of it.

When she opened her eyes, her body filled with icy cold and she saw Ezra Cooper's ghost standing near the big trees, translucent, see-through.

They made eye contact with each other and Lin's heart contracted with a wave of almost overwhelming grief.

A single tear, glistening in the moonlight, rolled down Ezra's cheek ... and then the ghost was gone.

8

White, cream, champagne-colored, and some blush pink long dresses hung on a rack in the boutique like ball gowns from a fantasy story. One by one, Lin and Viv slowly moved the hangers to see each dress more clearly.

"How are we going to choose our wedding dresses? Every one of these is gorgeous." Viv's blue eyes wandered over each of the gowns, some simple in cut and decoration, others more elaborate with sequins, crystals, and lace, and many in-between styles in fanciness.

"What sort of dress did you have in mind?" Lin asked. "Have you thought about the style or color you want?"

"I've flipped through bridal magazines, but I

haven't thought about the details of what I want it to look like. Have you?"

"Not really. I thought maybe a soft, off-white color? Not blinding white. But I'm not sure."

A woman came over to help them and the cousins explained about their fall double wedding.

"That's great. How exciting and fun." The woman's name tag said *Sherry* on it. "What styles have you thought of?"

"We have no idea," Lin revealed.

"I'll show you some different styles and choices of color that would go nicely with your physiques and builds," Sherry said. "Where will the wedding be?"

"We're having it at the Yacht Club in September. We've already reserved the date. We have the big ballroom, the terrace off the ballroom, and the gardens," Viv explained.

Sherry nodded. "Such a lovely place." The woman chose four dresses from the rack and handed two to Lin and two to Viv. "Would you like to start with these? Have you picked anything out that you like? While you're trying these on, I'll gather some more and bring the gowns to the dressing rooms for you. There are big mirrors on the far wall."

With Sherry's help, Lin and Viv spent forty-five minutes trying on wedding dresses and standing in front of the mirror checking how they looked.

"I don't know." Viv turned from side to side. "I like all of them, but I haven't found the one that sort of pops for me."

"I feel the same way." Lin pulled her hair up into a loose bun. "Any of these would be great, but I want to try on some more before I decide."

"We can check out another place, if you want to," Viv suggested.

Lin smiled. "There's a huge selection here. If we go somewhere else, it will make me more confused than I am now."

They tried on more gowns and when Viv stepped to the mirror this time, she and Lin both said at the same time, "This is the one."

The off-white satin dress had cap sleeves, a v-neck, and tiny pearls all over the bodice. It looked like it had been designed and made just for Viv.

"Gosh." Viv stared at herself in the mirror. "It's perfect."

Sherry hurried over carrying a long, delicate lace veil with French lace edging and used the attached comb to slip it into Viv's hair.

"Wow, look at that," Viv said softly. "The veil is the finishing touch."

"You look beautiful," Lin gazed at her cousin with a loving expression. "It's just right."

Sherry brought over a few pairs of earrings for Viv to try while Lin returned to the dressing room to put on a different gown.

Sherry helped her out of the one she was wearing and into the next dress, and when Lin looked in the mirror, she knew she'd found her wedding gown. The pearl white, sleeveless dress had a scoop neck, a lace bodice with tiny leaves and tendrils embroidered in the fabric, and yards of soft chiffon billowing from the waist to the floor, simple and elegant.

Lin blinked at her reflection and imagined Jeff standing by her side in his tuxedo, and then her vision began to swim and a different couple could be seen in the mirror.

Standing together with their backs to Lin, a young man wearing an eighteenth-century suit and a young woman dressed in a simple white gown trimmed with delicate lace held hands and faced a minister. A few people stood on each side watching, but Lin couldn't make out their faces.

The man slipped a gold band onto the bride's

ring finger as she held a bouquet of flowers in her right hand, and then he leaned in for a sweet and tender kiss.

Seeing the side of his face, Lin knew the groom was Ezra Cooper. The bride must be Abigail.

Lin's heart was light with the joy that floated from the happy couple, and the corners of her lips went up as she watched them complete the wedding ceremony.

When Ezra caught Lin's eye for a millisecond, she could feel a momentary flash of sorrow as if the man knew what lay ahead for them. She wished she could reach out and warn them of what fate had in store so she could change the course of their lives. She lifted her hand, reaching forward and when her fingertips touched the mirror, the vision disappeared into wisps of white smoke that floated gently away.

"No," Lin whispered.

Viv turned around and looked pointedly at her cousin, concerned that something was amiss. "Lin?"

"I'm fine. I got a little woozy for a second."

"I'll get you some juice. Trying things on can be tiring." Sherry hurried away.

"Are you sure you're fine?" Viv's eyes narrowed.

Lin gave a nod and held the chiffon skirt to the side. "What do you think?"

Viv said sincerely, "I think you look like some kind of a fairy princess. It looks beautiful on you."

"I think we both have found our gowns." Lin forced a smile.

Sherry returned with two glasses of juice and some cookies for the cousins.

"I feel better already," Lin reassured the shop owner. "Thank you."

The woman found a finger-tip length veil with tiny crystal beads sewed along the edge that clipped to Lin's bun. The veil complemented the style of the dress and completed the elegant picture.

Sherry said she couldn't believe the cousins had found their wedding gowns so quickly downplaying the fact they'd been in the store for three hours. The dresses and veils were paid for and arrangements were made for the cousins to return for minor alterations once they had purchased the shoes they would wear.

"Oh, gosh," Viv said with a shake of her head. "I forgot we have to choose shoes, too."

"Not today. Let's do that another time," Lin suggested. "I'm exhausted."

The young women went down to the docks and found a bench to sit on by the water.

"Who knew trying on dresses could wear you

out?" Lin pulled a clasp out of her hair and let it tumble loosely over her shoulders.

"What was going on in there when you spaced out at the mirror?" Viv eyed her cousin with suspicion.

Lin explained what she saw in the mirror and how her emotions swung from joy to sadness, and that she had an overwhelming urge to warn Ezra and Abigail.

"It's far too late for that, I'm afraid." Viv let out a long sigh. "Was Ezra in the room? Did you feel cold?"

"No. It seemed to be just a vision. I had no sense he was in the shop. I didn't see him. I didn't feel his presence around me. What I saw in the mirror must have been a vision from the past, it was Ezra's and Abigail's wedding day. I must have picked up on it because we were trying on dresses for our own weddings."

"That makes sense." Viv tapped the side of her face with her index finger. "Or does it?"

Lin chuckled. "I'm not sure much of anything makes sense these days. What does Ezra want from me? The fall his wife took doesn't seem to have been from foul play, at least nothing like that was implied in the short news announcement we found in the library or from what Anton found."

"I guess you'll have to watch and wait. Ezra will give you another hint." Viv teased her cousin. "Especially if he senses you don't have a clue what's going on with him."

"I really *don't* know what's going on with him." Lin's shoulders drooped. "I don't know how to help him."

"Maybe there isn't anything to do. Maybe Ezra just wanted to communicate with someone who can see ghosts ... someone who was also empathetic and understanding of his wife's accidental death and the terrible loss he endured."

Lin nodded. "The poor man. And poor Abigail. She and Ezra had everything going for them and then she lost her life, and the household became a den of sadness."

"When you had the vision, could you see what Abigail looked like?"

Lin looked out over the boats in the harbor. "Only from the back, and a little from the side. Her hair was a soft, sandy blond color. I couldn't make out her eye color. She was slender, but not skinny, and despite her short height, I got the fleeting feeling that Abigail could take care of herself very well." Lin clasped her hands in her lap. "I could also feel the love they had for each other, and knowing what they'd lost covered me in sadness. Last night in the cemetery standing by their graves, I felt the heaviness of Ezra's sorrow there, too."

"Why doesn't Abigail appear to you?" Viv asked.

Lin gave the slightest of shrugs. "That's a very good question. And one that doesn't appear to have a good answer."

9

When Lin and Jeff carried the folding chairs from the parking lot down to Jetties Beach, they saw Leonard waving to them from halfway down the sand.

"Everyone's here already," Lin noticed as they approached their group of friends, everyone arranging their chairs in a semi-circle to face the stage.

On the north side of Nantucket on the sound, Jetties Beach was a popular place with summer tourists for its gentle surf, large jetty, restaurant, restrooms, a café, and a large parking lot. Kayaks and sailboats could be rented there and a children's playground was tucked off to the side.

Leonard, Heather, Lori, the Snows, and Libby

and Anton sat down to chat before the music started. As part of the music festival, Viv and John's band would be playing prior to a well-known pop-rock band took the stage. There was still an hour to go before the concert start-time.

Lin placed her chair next to Heather's niece, Lori Michaels, and Jeff went over to talk with the Snows.

"How are things going?" Lin asked. "Are you enjoying living on the island and working in Heather's law office?"

"I am. The island is incredibly beautiful. I can hardly believe I'm living here." Lori had her dark blond hair plaited into a braid. She had on jeans, a checked blue shirt, and a navy pullover. The young woman had an easy, friendly way about her.

"Are you living with Heather?" Lin asked.

Lori nodded. "She has an accessory apartment at the back of her house. I'm all settled in. You told me the other day that you left the island for a few years. What were you doing while you were gone?"

"I went to the mainland for college and after that, I was working as a software developer. I'd been dating the same guy for a few years and we broke up. My grandfather owned a cottage here and when he passed away, he left the house to me. I was ready to come home," Lin said with a smile. "Where did you grow up?"

"Outside of Boston. My parents are still there. I was working in Boston and was ready for a change when Heather invited me to come work with her. I visited the island with my mom and dad when I was little. The beaches are the best here."

Lori kicked off her sandals and pushed her feet into the sand. "I was about ten when we came over for a week and ever since that trip, I dream about the island. It's always the same dream. I dream it a couple of times a week, sometimes more. I'm in town walking around the stores, looking in the shop windows. It's evening and the air is warm. After I go down to the docks to see the boats, I walk home. The house I'm in is so beautiful and peaceful. I'm so happy there. I walk through the rooms. They're decorated with such nice furniture, rugs, soft lighting. Right before I wake up, I'm standing in a hidden room, it's sort of a secret room that has a window that looks down to a room on the first floor. A woman is sitting in a rocking chair facing away from me. She's looking out a window at the water."

With a grin, Lori shifted in her beach chair and looked at Lin. "That's the end of the dream."

"Do you know the house in your dream? Did you stay in it when you were younger?"

Lori shook her head. "I don't know the house. I never see the outside of the house in my dream, not even the neighborhood or the street. The inside is big, but I've never been in it in real life." The young woman smiled. "I feel like I know the place from wandering around inside of it in my dreams. Heather told me sometimes there are house tours on the island. I'll have to sign up when one of them is offered. Maybe I'll find the house from my dreams." Lori picked up a handful of sand and let it slip through her fingers like the tiny particles were inside an hourglass. "Do you ever dream the same dream?"

Lin felt uncomfortable. "I used to when I was little."

"What did you dream?"

"I dreamt about being bullied. When I was in elementary school, a girl I thought was a friend, told a lie about me. It was mean. It made me feel ... helpless and betrayed."

Lori's face fell. "Do you still dream it?"

With a shake of her head, Lin said, "No. It's gone. It stopped after I moved back here."

"I hope mine doesn't stop because I moved here. I love that dream." Lori leaned closer to Lin.

"Leonard seems really nice. Heather likes him. Are you and Leonard related?"

Lin was surprised to hear the question. "No, we're friends ... and business partners. He *is* nice. I'm glad to see Leonard and Heather enjoying themselves together."

"Heather needs someone. She works way too much, has always been so focused on her career and her charitable interests. Leonard is good for her."

Lin asked the young woman about studying law.

"As an undergraduate, I studied history. Colonial America and early American history were my favorite periods. I also love the old houses, the sea captain's houses, the gardens. I decided to go to law school." Lori grinned. "And unlike many of my colleagues, I loved everything about the study of law. I'm drawn to it for some reason."

"You're lucky you found what you enjoy doing," Lin said with a nod. "Are you married?"

"Oh, gosh, no. I can't even find a boyfriend." Lori laughed. "I date plenty, but nobody is a good match. It's discouraging. I feel like I'll never find the right person." She asked Lin about Jeff and the wedding plans. "It sounds great. Where are you having the ceremony itself?"

Lin said, "At the yacht club, I guess. We haven't

gone over the logistics yet."

"Plenty of time to figure it out," Lori said. "I think I'll go get a drink at the restaurant. Want anything?"

Lin declined and Lori and Heather went off across the sand to the restaurant to bring some food and drinks back to the group.

Leonard came over and sat down in Lori's beach chair. "How's it going, Coffin?"

"Pretty good. Viv and I picked out our wedding dresses yesterday."

"Surprised there were any dresses left, the two of you waited long enough to get them."

With a chuckle, Lin said, "It's not late at all. It's only April. The wedding isn't for five months. I took pictures of Viv and me in the dresses." She was about to pull out her phone. "Want to see them?"

"Nope. I want to be surprised."

"Really?" Lin wasn't expecting that answer. "Want me to *tell* you about the dresses?"

"No. I want to see them for the first time at the wedding. I *am* invited, right?"

"Yes, you're invited. And you're not the groom, you know, so it's okay if you see the dresses before the wedding."

"I don't want to see them. I told you I want to be surprised. It's bad luck."

"I didn't know you were so superstitious," Lin teased.

Leonard sighed. "I saw Marguerite's dress before the wedding. It was bad luck."

"Oh." Lin's heart contracted with sadness.

Years ago, Leonard's wife, Marguerite, died in a car crash on the mainland when she went to interview for a job. The loss of his wife sent the man into a tailspin that lasted for years, and he didn't pull out of it until he and Lin became friends and business partners.

The similarities between Ezra and Leonard suddenly struck Lin. Both men lost their young wives to accidents, both men fell into the depths of misery and depression after their wives died. Ezra succumbed to his grief, and Leonard might have done the same if he and Lin hadn't become close to one another.

"So don't show me the dresses." Leonard looked out at the darkening sea. "I know its foolishness, but I'm not taking any chances."

"Okay," Lin told him, and after a few moments of silence she said, "Heather's nice."

Leonard looked at Lin and rolled his eyes. "Yes, she is. Don't give me the third degree about her, Coffin. We're taking things slow. Leave it at that."

"If it was *me* who was dating someone new, you'd ask me questions about it."

"Yes, I would, but this is different. You're young, I'm old."

Lin stared at her friend. "I don't know what on earth age has to do with anything."

A sly smile crossed Leonard's lips. "I brought it up as a trick to keep you from cross-examining me."

"It won't work," Lin told him.

"I didn't think it would. I'll have to think of something else."

"I'm your friend. You're supposed to tell me stuff."

"I tell you plenty." Leonard saw Heather and Lori coming from the beach restaurant struggling with the containers of drinks and food and he jumped to his feet to go and help them.

Lin thought about how hard it must have been for Leonard and Ezra to go through the loss of their spouses. She was happy that Leonard was turning his life towards happiness after so many years of suffering.

But what about Ezra?

Why are you trying to communicate with me? What's changed now?

What do you want me to do?

10

Lin was doing spring clean-up by raking up the old leaves and lawn debris in the yard of the Snows' three-story, white Colonial mansion and art gallery on the corner of Main Street. Crocuses and tulips bloomed in the flowerbed by the white picket fence in the front of the yard. Lin knelt and used her hand to pull out dried up leaves from in-between the spring flowers.

"Everything's looking great." Robert Snow came out of the gallery to speak with Lin. "Spring has finally sprung." Robert, his wife, Lila, son, Roy, daughter-in-law, Suzanne, and young grandson, Chase, lived in the huge house together.

Lin stood to greet the man. "And not a moment too soon."

"Are you almost done? How about a cup of tea before you head off to your next client?"

"I'd love that. Shall I come into the gallery once I finish up?"

"I'll put the kettle on." Robert hurried back inside.

The man was pouring hot water into two mugs when Lin came through the door. She kicked off her work boots so as not to track mud into the gallery. Robert handed her the steaming tea and they sat in the two easy chairs at the back of the shop.

"The concert was wonderful. We were very impressed with your cousin's band. They were terrific." Robert took a careful sip from his mug.

"Viv and John have been playing for years. They write a lot of their own music. I think they deserve more attention for their skills, but it's tough to get a break, and anyway, they're both happy with their day jobs. It was a fun evening at the beach concert. A little chilly by the water on an April night, but it was all good."

They chatted about the tourist season kicking into gear soon, town happenings, and what Robert wanted the yard to look like this year.

"Have you thought about the flowers you'd like planted?" Lin asked.

"Lila has some ideas. I'll leave it to her. She'll talk with you next time you come by," Robert said. "She's out at a meeting." The man checked to be sure a customer wasn't about to come in and then he leaned forward. "How's Tim Pierce's table?"

"It's been quiet." Lin told Robert how Libby, she, and Anton tried the tipping tables game. "The ghost's name is Ezra Cooper. He was a mason in the late 1700s. He owned Tim's house. Not only did Ezra give us his name by making the table tap, but I saw him the other night when Viv and I were leaving Tim's house."

Robert almost leapt from his chair. "You saw him?"

Lin nodded. "Only briefly. A few seconds, and then he was gone. But I know it was him. He was on the opposite sidewalk across from Tim's house on the far side of the street."

"Remarkable." Robert's eyes were keen with interest. "Are you able to communicate with one another?"

"No, well, only with the table tipping and tapping. I have to guess at clues. The ghosts never speak to me."

"It must make it very difficult," Robert observed.

"It's hard to know what they want me to do." Lin

glanced around the gallery. "Has Captain Baker been around?"

"Lila and I have sensed his presence a few times over the past couple of days." Robert smiled. "He seems to be in a good mood."

"I wondered if the captain knew Ezra Cooper. They both lived in town in the late 1700s."

Robert's eyes widened. "I could ask him, I suppose, but he's never communicated with us other than by smashing or throwing things. I wouldn't know how I'd get an answer from him."

"Oh, yes, I know. I didn't think we'd be able to get an answer. The thought crossed my mind that the men might have known one another back then, in passing anyway. It's strange, isn't it? Here we are hundreds of years later and both of them remain on the island as ghosts."

"I often wonder why the captain stays here and doesn't cross over." Robert's forehead lined in concentration. "I know he loves this house. I know the terrible tragedy he suffered. But why stay? Why linger on the earthly plane?"

Lin held her hands up in a gesture of helplessness. "I wish I knew. Is it because this place was home? Because it's a comforting place to be? Are the spirits clinging to the place because it seems safe? Because it's a known entity?"

"Why doesn't another spirit come and help them cross?" Robert questioned.

Lin could only shake her head. "I don't know what Ezra wants from me. There doesn't seem to be a mystery to solve that will allow him to feel released from his worry or concern. It doesn't seem he was wronged in any way. We haven't found anything amiss yet besides his wife's accident ... and there's nothing I can do about that."

"When was the last time you saw him?"

"I saw him across from Tim's house a few nights ago," Lin said. "Viv and I were shopping for our wedding gowns the day before yesterday. I had a vision of Ezra and his wife at their own wedding. I don't think the vision was caused by Ezra because I didn't get cold ... no icy air surrounded me." She shrugged. "I don't know how the vision came to me."

Robert was quiet for a moment. "I can't even come up with a theory about how you saw the vision." He took in a deep breath. "If Abigail Cooper's fall was the result of an attack or foul play, how would you know?"

"We try to find old articles or a letter or something

that reports the incident. If it was mentioned in a letter, the writer might say something about Abigail being attacked or pushed or whatever. Without some written record, we're only going on speculation. And at this point, we aren't thinking Abigail's fall was anything more than an accident. No news report, no nothing."

Returning from her meeting, Lila came into the gallery from the back staircase and she sat with Robert and Lin as they told her about their discussion.

"Perhaps the man is just lonely," she said. "Ezra might not be able to let go of the past and so he stays behind and doesn't want to cross. Maybe he can't come to terms with what happened to his wife."

"But why is Ezra more upset over things than he has been in the past? Why now? What's different?" Lin questioned. "Why has the table been tapping crazily? What does Ezra want that he didn't want in years past?"

"I would think he's wanted the same thing all these years," Lila guessed. "I don't know what that could be."

"To go back in time and keep the accident from happening?" Robert offered.

Lin sat up, blinking. "To go back in time...."

"Ezra's ghost must certainly know you don't have

a time travel machine," Robert said. "He can't be asking *that* of you. I simply meant that going back to the late 1700s is the only way the accident could be avoided. Ezra knows that, and if he could go back in time, he would have done it already."

Lila said, "Ezra might be content here. Maybe he doesn't want anything at all."

"Why all the hubbub in Tim's house then?" Robert pointed out. "If Ezra was happy here, he wouldn't have been causing the antique table to rock and sway and tap."

"True," Lila admitted.

"Let's concentrate on what's changed from previous years." Lin tried to think logically. "Tim's grandfather passed away, for one."

"Tim took over his grandfather's house. He moved here from Boston," Robert added.

Lila asked, "Do you think Ezra doesn't like Tim? Is that why Ezra has been so agitated? Maybe he doesn't like the fact that Tim is now the owner."

"Why would Ezra be bothered by that? Ezra doesn't know much about Tim," Robert said. "Tim is only going to maintain the place, keep it in tip-top condition. What could Ezra not like about Tim?"

"Well, maybe Ezra is sad about the grandfather passing," Lila told them.

Robert said, "If that's the case, then why doesn't Ezra cross over. That way, he might be able to see the grandfather again."

"Maybe the man's death is what's upsetting Ezra," Lin said. "It might remind him of the loss of his wife and it might cause him to relive the grief he suffered."

Robert shook his head. "I don't think that's it. It's been what? More than two hundred years since Abigail and Ezra Cooper died. Ezra's ghost must have been in the house since he passed away. Of all the other people who have owned that house, some of them must have died. Why didn't Ezra get upset over those deaths?"

"Maybe he did," Lila speculated. "But maybe he didn't have someone like Lin to communicate his distress to."

The Snows looked at Lin.

"Is it me?" Lin's mouth dropped open. "Is me being on the island the reason? Is Ezra trying to tell me about his anger and sorrow? Has he never had anyone to share his grief with?"

"That's about as good a reason as any," Robert agreed.

"Perhaps Ezra doesn't want anything from you,"

Lila told Lin. "Maybe all he wants is for someone to validate his feelings."

"That would sure be easy enough." Lin rubbed at the kink at the base of her neck. "It's possible that all I have to do is listen and acknowledge Ezra's feelings." Letting out a sigh, she asked, "Why do I think there's more to this than that?"

Robert's face brightened as he turned to Lin. "Why don't you ask the table? Ask if Ezra wants something more than your understanding. Ezra might be able to communicate via the table taps. He told you his name with the tapping. He might be able to tell you something more."

With a hint of a smile, Lin sat straighter. "Why haven't I thought to do that? I'll call Libby later today."

11

Libby, Lin, and Nicky walked through the dark streets of town on the way to Lin's house. The dog stopped every now and then to sniff at the edge of a lawn or at the base of a tree and the women paused and waited for him before they moved on.

"When I talked with the Snows, we wondered if Ezra just wants someone who can communicate with him and understand his loss," Lin told Libby.

Libby had a skeptical look on her face. "But you can't really communicate with him."

"Not verbally, but over time, I get a sense of what a ghost wants. They know I can see them. They aren't invisible anymore. They aren't just lost amongst the living. I relate to them. They know I'm sympathetic to them."

Nicky glanced up at Lin and let out a soft woof.

"You have a point." Libby reached down and patted Nicky on the head. "Maybe there isn't anything you need to help Ezra with. He may be happy there's someone who is able to acknowledge him. We'll see if he can tell us anything through the table."

"Viv is going to meet us at the house. She'll take down the letters while we sit at the table and ask the questions."

Libby said, "I've been working with some friends to try and find some information on Ezra and Abigail Cooper. So far we haven't discovered any more than what Anton found about the couple ... only the birth documents, the marriage certificate, and the death notices. Records back then were spotty or nonexistent, or they've been lost to time. Unfortunately, there may not be any more information left to find."

As they walked up the brick sidewalks and turned into Lin's neighborhood, Lin brought up Abigail Cooper.

"Why doesn't she appear to me?"

"Abigail may have crossed over after she died," Libby pointed out. "Ezra's grief may have prevented him from leaving the island. He stays here agonizing over his loss. He may be unable to cross over due to feeling he was never able to finish living his life on earth."

"It's so complicated." Lin turned the lock on her front door.

"Life and death can be very complicated," Libby said.

Lin made tea and cut slices of cake and the women took the refreshments out to the deck. A mist rose from the meadow behind the cottage making it look mysterious and a little spooky in the moonlit night.

Libby asked about the wedding plans and Lin filled her in on the details.

"I'm very much looking forward to it," Libby said. "It will be a beautiful and meaningful day and I can't wait for it to come."

"We're here." Viv called and came into the house with Queenie who padded over to the dog and licked his ears. Viv poured some tea and carried her mug out to the deck. "Give me a few minutes before we start. The bookstore has been crazy today. This is the first time I've sat down."

Watching Nicky and Queenie heading to the meadow, she said, "Oh, look at the field. It looks like ghosts are floating on the moonlight over the mist. It's creepy." She shuddered, and then sighed. "But I suppose it's fitting for our purpose tonight." Viv suddenly looked hopeful. "Unless you've changed your minds about the table tipping?"

"The plan is the same," Lin confided. "You can sit across the room far away from us like last time."

"How about I sit out here and you tip the table inside?" Viv kidded. "You can shout the number of taps through the screen door."

Libby stood. "Shall we?"

"Already?" Viv groaned.

"No time like the present." Libby led the way inside where she and Lin set up the tilt table and moved two chairs next to it.

Viv took a seat at the kitchen island with her pen and pad of paper. "Whenever you're ready. Let's get this over with."

Lin dimmed the lights and when she sat down across from Libby, they both placed their palms on the edge of the table and sat in silence for almost five full minutes.

"Ezra?" Lin asked softly. "I need help understanding how I can assist you. I need help understanding what you need. Can you tell us something that can lead me in the right direction? What do you need, Ezra? Is there something I can do for you? Is there something I can find for you?"

Nothing happened for quite a while and the women waited patiently, not wanting to rush the spirit, and then a wave of icy air enveloped Lin and she began to feel almost lightheaded. As the room started to spin, she pressed harder against the table trying to steady herself with her hands.

The table began to bobble a little as if the legs were uneven, and Libby and Lin held their breath.

The antique piece lifted an inch off the floor, tipped to one side, and began hammering the floor with one of its legs.

Viv stared with a look of horror, but she counted the taps ... ten, eleven, twelve.

The table stopped for a half minute and then started up again.

Fourteen, fifteen. A long pause.

It went through the sequence of pausing and tapping two more times, and then it floated back down to the floor and went quiet.

"Is it over?" Viv whispered.

"I think so," Lin said. "Right before it started, I got cold and my head felt dizzy. I feel back to normal again now."

"What was the message?" Libby asked.

Viv looked down at her pad and filled in the letters that corresponded with the number of taps. Her head popped up.

"What did Ezra spell?" Lin questioned.

Viv's eyes met Libby's and then Lin's. "He spelled ... love."

Lin hurried over to her cousin and stared at the word on the paper. "What does he mean?"

Viv shrugged. "Your guess is as good as mine."

"Are you sure you counted the taps correctly?" Lin asked.

Viv made a face. "It wasn't that hard. It was four letters, not a whole paragraph of information."

"Love? What does that mean?" Lin ran her hand over her hair. "How can I do anything about that?"

"Does he mean the love he lost when his wife died?" Viv questioned.

"If he does mean that, what can I do to help him?" Lin's face was blank.

"Can you help him come to terms with his loss?" Libby suggested. "Is that what he wants help with?"

Suddenly, with a bang, the top of the antique tilt table flipped itself up vertically and locked itself in place.

The three woman were wide eyed and Viv was gripping her cousin's arm.

"Yikes. Why the heck did that happen?" Viv's voice was barely audible.

Lin's heart was pounding. "I don't think Ezra liked what we were saying about coming to terms with his loss."

"Why don't we sit outside," Libby nodded to the screen door.

The air was growing chilly when they took seats around the teak deck table. Nicky and Queenie emerged from the meadow and sat on the deck looking out at the darkness.

"So what is going on?" Viv leaned closer and kept her voice down. "Ezra doesn't want help with dealing with his grief?"

"It seems not." Lin took a quick look to the door leading to the kitchen.

"Well, what does he want then?" Viv asked with an exasperated tone.

Libby's eyes were narrowed as she attempted to make some sense of the experience. "Before we started, Lin asked what Ezra needed, if there was something she could do for him, if there was something she could find for him."

"That's right." Lin nodded.

"He answered your question," Viv told her. "He said he needs love."

"What can I do about that?"

Viv raised an eyebrow. "Maybe he wants you to play matchmaker and find him an available ghost."

Lin groaned and looked to Libby. "Do you have a better idea?"

The older woman took a moment to answer. "Ezra wants love. He lost his wife and then he lost his will to live. The couple's life was ruined by a simple accident, a twist of fate." She looked at Lin. "Can you help him cross over? He might be able to reunite with Abigail on the other side."

Lin's mouth hung open. "How can I help him cross?"

"Other ghosts have crossed after you helped them with something."

"But I don't know what Ezra wants," Lin said helplessly. "Tapping out the word *love* doesn't give me anything to go on. He must know how to cross over. If he was ready to go, he'd go. He must realize that Abigail is probably on the spirit plane, whatever that is," Lin mumbled. "He needs something to happen here before he'll cross."

"But what is it?" Viv questioned. "Like I say every time, can't these ghosts be more specific about things? Sheesh. You see ghosts. You're not a mind reader."

Lin frowned. "I don't know what to do."

Libby let out a long sigh. "Let's table this for a while."

With a slight grin, Viv eyed the woman. "*Table*? Did you say *table* this for a while?"

Lin couldn't help but chuckle.

Libby rolled her eyes at the cousins. "I'll put it another way. Let's put on hold trying to figure out what Ezra wants. Maybe something new will develop that will help us understand what he needs. Let's give it some time and see where things lead."

"I don't think we have a choice," Lin agreed reluctantly. "Anyway, I think the table is done with us. I get the feeling it isn't going to do any more tapping. I'll ask Tim if we can return it."

12

Leonard held the drawing of the landscape design work planned for Tim Pierce's backyard and he pointed to the bed on the right side of the property.

"That bed needs to be widened to fit the plants that are going in there."

Lin went over and used the shovel to mark how far out it needed to go. "Like this?"

"Yeah, good."

Nicky sat at Leonard's feet looking sleepy from the sun and the warm temperature.

Most of the beds had been marked out and two of the former flower beds that were choked with weeds had been cleaned up. Lin and Leonard, with the dog supervising, had spent most of the morning laying things out. The afternoon would be spent removing more weeds and dead plants.

"Let's take a break and eat lunch," Leonard suggested.

"You don't have to ask me twice."

Lin spread a blanket in the shade of a tree and she and her partner and Nicky sat down and the lunch boxes were opened. Leonard had some leftover stew in his thermos and a piece of chunky bread. "I made cornbread last night. Have some if you like." He put the container on the blanket.

"You bet I'd like." Lin bit into the cornbread and closed her eyes for a moment. "Heavenly. Be careful or I'll eat all of it." She opened her lunch box and removed a focaccia sandwich of mushrooms, eggplant, onions, tomatoes, and cheese, and a bowl to put Nicky's dog food in. "I brought some cookies for us, but they aren't as tasty as the cornbread."

"Tell me about the séance you had last night." Leonard spooned some stew into his mouth.

"It wasn't a séance."

"Same thing. What happened?"

Lin gave her friend a report on the previous evening's adventure. "So the takeaway is that I have no idea what Ezra wants."

"It was a useful way to spend your time then," Leonard teased.

"I don't know what to do."

Nicky crawled over and rested his head on Lin's lap.

"Every time you get a new ghost you always say that. You'll figure it out, Coffin. Don't push."

"If I don't push, I'll never get the answers." Lin reached into the container of cornbread. "I need another piece."

"It isn't good to stress eat," Leonard warned her.

"I'm not stress eating. I'm eating because it tastes good. It's your fault." She bit into the second square of cornbread. "There's Tim." She nodded towards the back of the house.

"Hey." Tim walked over and sat down with Leonard and Lin, and patted Nicky behind the ears. "I see you've started on the yard."

"It's going to look great when it's done," Lin said. "How are things going for you working remotely and all?"

"It's fine." Tim looked around the yard. The young man didn't seem himself. He seemed tired and low energy like he hadn't slept for days."

"We're done with the tilt table. I don't think it

will bother you again. Shall I bring it back?" Lin asked.

Tim shrugged. "Sure. Whatever you want."

Nicky nudged the man's hand for more patting and he obliged.

"Are you enjoying the house?" Lin asked.

"Yeah, it's fine."

Leonard made eye contact with Lin and then he got up to go to the truck.

"Is everything okay?" Lin questioned.

Tim nodded. "Yeah, everything's fine."

"Then why does it seem like everything *isn't* fine?"

Tim's shoulders slumped. "I don't know. I'm feeling ... sort of ... lonely."

"Do you have friends on-island?"

"I don't. Most of my friends are in Boston or on the west coast."

"Have you been back to the city?"

"Not yet."

"How do you spend your day?" Lin asked.

"I work most of the day, then I make dinner and go to bed."

Lin's eyebrows went up. "You need to get out and meet people. You can't hole up in the house alone. What about hobbies you like? You can connect with people through your hobbies. And what about some charity work? You can meet people by volunteering a couple of times a week somewhere."

"I haven't had the time."

"You need to make the time," Lin said quietly. "You can't live somewhere without having a social network."

"I know I need to do those things." Tim ran his hand over his face. "I've been so tired. I don't have the energy."

"Is it because you recently lost your grandfather?"

"That's probably part of it, but it's certainly not most of it. I don't know what's wrong with me. It's like I've run out of gas."

"It's a bunch of change in a short time," Lin said. "It can have a negative effect on a person. Even when good things cause the change, it can sap a person of their energy."

"I guess that makes sense."

"Listen, some friends and I are planning to go on a bike ride this weekend. Why don't you come with us?" Lin asked.

"I don't have a bike."

"My fiancé has extra bikes and helmets. He can bring one for you. How about it? Everyone is nice.

You'll like them. It's always a good time. We usually go out for drinks and appetizers after the ride."

Tim nodded. "Okay. I'd like to come. Thanks."

Lin smiled broadly. "Great. Give me your number and I'll text you about the time and place to meet." Tim told her his number and she punched it into her phone.

"Thanks, Lin. See you soon."

When Tim went inside the house, Leonard wandered back from the truck.

"I thought Tim might open up if he was talking only to you. Did you get anything out of him? What's wrong?" Leonard asked.

"He's lonely." Lin made sure the man had disappeared into the house before speaking. "He seems sad and unsure if he made the right decision to move to Nantucket. He doesn't know anyone here and he works all the time."

"Not a good combination." Leonard gave Nicky a small piece of the cornbread.

"I invited him to come on the bike ride we're going on this weekend. It will get him out, he'll meet new people, and he'll get some exercise. We'll go out for drinks afterwards. I think it will do him good. Why don't you come, too?"

"You can count me out. I don't ride bikes."

"Why not? It's fun."

"Fun is sitting in the backyard in my Adirondack chair listening to the birds sing. I work hard all week. I don't need to ride around the island like a nut on two wheels."

Lin laughed. "Is that how everyone sees us?"

"It's how I see you."

"You should try it once. You might like biking."

Leonard gave her the eye and a frown-face. "It's not happening, Coffin. Come on, let's get back to work."

～

After work, Lin and Nicky walked to Viv's house for dinner and when they arrived, Queenie greeted them at the door and then she and the dog scampered outside to patrol the backyard.

"I'm making spaghetti." Viv stirred the pasta in the big pot on the stove. "I got back from the bookstore late and this will be easy and quick."

"Fine with me. You know I love spaghetti. I could eat it at every meal." Lin brushed some olive oil onto slices of bread before sprinkling them with some Parmesan cheese.

"How was work?" Viv asked.

"We were at Tim Pierce's house for most of the day. We just started clearing out the old growth and the weeds. Tim came out to talk to me for a while. I told him he could have the antique table back. I told him it was probably done bumping about, but he didn't ask anything about it. He had no interest in it at all. He's feeling sort of depressed."

Viv turned to her cousin, surprised to hear about Tim's low mood. "Why?"

Lin explained what he'd told her. "He's all alone here. He needs to get out and meet people. I invited him to bike with us this weekend."

Viv poured some wine into two glasses and handed one to Lin. She looked at her cousin pointedly. "Is something wrong with that house?"

"What house?"

"Tim's house. Is there a curse on it or something? Abigail and Ezra lived there and look at what happened to them. Did Tim's grandfather live there long?"

"I think he lived there since Tim was a young boy."

"Did anything bad happen to him?"

"I don't know. He lived to an old age."

"It must be that house. Did Tim seem really down? Do we need to check on him?" Viv asked.

"I think you're letting your imagination get away from you," Lin said. "Ezra and his wife ran into misfortune and Tim is feeling the effects of moving someplace where he doesn't know anyone so he's feeling lonely. Those things don't point to a curse. Anyway, there's no such thing."

"We don't know anything about the other people who have lived there. There might be more evidence to suggest something's wrong with that place. And why is it okay to believe in ghosts, but not in curses?"

Lin shook her head as she slipped the baking sheet of bread into the oven. "Because we've actually seen the ghosts. A curse is just made up nonsense."

"Is it? Don't some places seem like they're bad luck? Don't some families seem like they have a ton of bad luck?"

"I guess so, but it's not because of a curse."

"Okay, forget the curse idea and consider this ... there could be a spirit lingering in that house. An angry spirit who takes out its anger on the occupants of the house," Viv said.

Lin's face tensed at the suggestion. "That could be."

"Tim doesn't have a girlfriend? A partner?" Viv asked.

"No, he doesn't. At least, he's never mentioned anyone."

"Did he recently break up with someone? Is that why he's in a funk? Is that why he doesn't seem to have any interest in going out?"

"I don't know," Lin said. "That's a good idea though. If he left a relationship recently, that would be playing a part in making him feel low. That could also be why he was keen to move here. A fresh start in a new place. Starting over."

"When we go biking, ask him about his life," Viv suggested. "That way, we'll know what's going on with him." She gave her cousin the eye. "Then maybe we can decide if there's something dangerous in that house or not."

13

Lin, Jeff, Viv, John, Heather's niece, Lori, and some of the men's friends spent three hours biking around the island on the off-road bike lanes. The beautiful late afternoon was perfect for the ride with temperatures in the high-sixties and no wind. The island was coming to life with flowers blooming, the grass and marsh turning freshly green, and the new leaves unfurling on the trees.

The group rode past the white sand beaches, along wide paths through the woods, past the sea marshes, past Sankaty Lighthouse and Brant Point Lighthouse, and the lovely cottages and elegant mansions that lined the roads.

Lin was disappointed to hear from Tim that he wouldn't be able to participate in the bike ride as he had too much work. He promised to go the next time, and she hoped he meant it. It was important to get out, have a change of scenery, meet people and enjoy their company especially for someone new to the island.

The cyclists stopped in Madaket to get some snacks and replenish water bottles and to take a picture of the group. Lori was warm and friendly and got along so well with everyone it was like she'd been friends with them for years.

After the ride, the friends stopped at Lin's house for quick showers and a change of clothes, and then they headed into town for appetizers and drinks.

"That was great," Lori told Lin as they sipped drinks. "I'm so glad you invited me. It's nice to meet such a great group of people."

"Did you grow up in Massachusetts?" Lin asked the young woman.

"No, I lived outside of Chicago. I went to college and law school in California, then got a job in Boston. Heather offered me the job here a couple of months ago, but it took time to wrap things up and make the move."

"Did you come to the island often to visit?"

"My parents and sister and I came for a week each summer for about five years when we were in elementary school, but then my mom got a new job and my sister and I were in sports and activities so we vacationed closer to home. I did miss Nantucket though. I loved it here."

"Lin told me about your recurring dream of being in a big house on the island," Viv said. "When did that start?"

"It started after the first time we visited here. It's strange, isn't it? It's stuck with me ever since then."

"And you dream about it every week?" Viv questioned.

"At least once a week." Lori nodded.

Huge plates of nachos, baked potato skins, mini pizzas, and vegetable rollups were brought to the long table and Lori, Lin, and Viv took small plates and loaded them up with the food.

Lori asked about the fall wedding and the cousins told her the details about the day. Viv asked if Lori was seeing anyone.

"I'm not. I wish I was." Lori licked some melted cheese from her finger. "I date, but I can't seem to find the right guy. Maybe I need a matchmaker."

"Not being in a relationship made it easier for you to relocate to the island," Viv pointed out a benefit of Lori being single. With a smile, she added, "Maybe you'll find your match on Nantucket. I bet there's a guy on this island who's been waiting for you to show up."

Lori laughed. "That would be perfect. I just need to find him."

When Lin went off to get a new round of drinks, Viv asked Lori to describe the dream she'd had since childhood. "Do you mind telling me? I love this kind of stuff."

Viv and Lori sat on bar stools and Lori began her story.

"In the dream, I never see the neighborhood or the outside of the house. I'm inside wandering from room to room. I know every inch of the place, everything is familiar to me. There's a secret room on the second floor with a smaller door. The room is like a reading nook with a few comfortable chairs, a couple of lamps, and a big window that lets in a ton of light. There's another smaller window that looks down into a den on the first floor. A woman is sitting in a rocker and she's looking outside to the water."

"Do you know the woman?" Viv asked.

"No." Lori shook her head. "She seems familiar, but I can't see her face. She's looking away from me."

"Do you know the people who own the house in the dream?" Viv added some of the mini pizzas to her plate.

"I have no idea who owns the house." Lori gave an impish smile. "But I guess they don't mind me wandering around in their home."

"How do you feel when you're in the house? Are you scared?"

Lori's eyes widened. "Not at all. It's not like that. I love that house. I feel like I'm home, comfortable, happy, content, lighthearted. It's a wonderful feeling to be there ... like all of my worries have vanished and I know everything is just the way it's supposed to be."

Viv asked, "Are you sad when you wake up? Since everything is so perfect in the dream?"

"No, I'm happy. The feelings from the dream stay with me, for at least part of the day."

"But don't you feel sad that this house is fictional?"

Lori looked down at her glass and said softly, "I never thought the house wasn't real." She made eye contact with Viv. "I guess I always thought I'd find it someday." A half-smile formed on the young woman's mouth. "I suppose it's silly to think so."

"It's not silly at all." Viv smiled. "Maybe you know this house from somewhere you were when you were little."

Lori tilted her head to the side. "I wonder. I've always thought the house was on Nantucket."

"Do your parents know about the dream?"

"Oh, yes. It's a family joke."

"The house doesn't sound familiar to them?" Viv questioned.

"No, they don't know the place. It's not familiar to them at all."

Lin returned with a small tray of drinks. Having overheard part of their conversation, she said, "You'll just have to save your money, buy a lot, and build that house from your dreams."

"But, it's an old house," Lori protested.

"You can build a reproduction." Lin handed the drinks to Viv and Lori.

With a smile, Lori said, "I just might have to do that."

~

Lin and Viv walked up Main Street under the old-fashioned streetlamps heading for their homes after a fun evening at the pub with their friends.

"I like Lori. She's a nice addition to our group," Viv said.

"I think so, too. She's fun, easygoing, genuine.

She seems like a kind person." Lin yawned. "I'm feeling really tired. I'm looking forward to crawling into my comfy bed with Nicky by my side and doing a crossword puzzle before I fall asleep ... if I can stay awake long enough to do the puzzle."

"I should do some paperwork for the bookstore, but it's not going to happen." Viv glanced at her cousin. "What do you think about Tim not coming with us today? Was he just avoiding all of us?"

Lin shrugged. "Maybe he really did have too much work to do."

"Then I think he needs to hire some more help because working all the hours he does during the week is not healthy, not mentally and not physically. Tim's going to run himself into the ground, and then what will he do?"

"I agree. It's one thing to work hard. It's another thing to work twenty-four, seven. He can't keep up that pace. He'll be miserable."

"I hope Tim isn't feeling so low that he canceled today. I hope that's not the reason he didn't come."

"That thought crossed my mind, too." Lin said. "If he's depressed, he might not have the energy to drag himself out of the house and interact with people he doesn't know."

"It's late or I'd tell you to text him."

"I'm going to see him tomorrow. I'm bringing the table back to the Colonial. I'll see how he's doing then."

"Good. That makes me feel better. I worry about him," Viv admitted.

Lin gave her cousin an affectionate squeeze. "You're a good person."

"Have you seen your ghost lately?" Viv asked.

"Not recently."

"Maybe he'll show up soon and give you a clue about what he wants."

"I sure hope so."

The young women hugged at the corner of Main Street and said goodnight as Viv turned right and Lin took the road to the left.

"See you tomorrow for dinner." Viv waved and disappeared into the darkness.

Lin's mind was at work thinking about the day with friends, worrying about Tim Pierce, and going over details having to do with her ghost when she turned down her street and felt oddly chilly.

It wasn't the cold from the evening air and it didn't feel like the icy whoosh that surrounded her whenever a ghost was making an appearance.

This sensation was different and difficult to

describe. She realized the chilly feeling didn't cover her entire body, it was only at her back.

Fear gripped Lin's stomach and she took a quick glance behind her.

No one was there.

She listened for the sound of footsteps.

No one walked nearby.

Feeling oddly vulnerable, Lin picked up her pace, and when she could see her house in the distance, she ran.

Pulling the key from her pocket as she dashed down the lane, she jammed it into the lock and flung the door open. Breathing hard, she slammed it shut and locked the door.

As she turned around, Nicky woofed and she almost jumped out of her skin.

The dog was sitting there watching her with his tail tapping against the floor.

"Nick. You scared me." With her hand over her heart, Lin knelt and gave him a hug. "Good boy. I'm glad to be home. Foolish me. When I was walking, I let my mind race and I got myself worked up over nothing." Lin let out a sigh of relief. "Come on, Nick, let's go sit in the bedroom and do a crossword puzzle."

14

After her workday was done, Lin placed the antique tilt table into her van and drove over to Tim's house. When he opened the door, he looked surprised for a second.

"Oh, gosh, I forgot you were coming. Sorry. I got so wrapped up in my work."

"That's okay. Here's the table. I don't think it will bother you anymore."

"Great. Thanks." Tim lifted the table from the front steps and set it down in the foyer. "Come in."

"That's okay," Lin said. "I don't want to keep you."

"I'd like a break, if you have time for some coffee or tea."

Lin accepted the invitation and went with Tim to

the kitchen where he bustled around preparing the beverages.

"How was the bike ride? I was sorry I had to miss it."

"It was a nice day. Come with us next time, if you can." Lin sat at the kitchen island.

"I really want to. Something came up and I had to address it." Tim filled a small pitcher with cream and placed a sugar bowl on the island along with two silver spoons. He poured coffee into the cups and set one down in front of his guest.

"How's the work going?" Lin asked as she poured some cream into her coffee.

"It's never ending. I need to learn to set parameters." Tim took a seat next to Lin.

"That will help, otherwise it's impossible to get your head above water. Leonard and I have to turn some potential clients away because we don't have the time and it's hard to find good, reliable workers. We want to do it all, but we've learned it isn't a good idea to spread ourselves too thin."

"I also have to get used to working remotely," Tim said. "It's not as easy as it sounds."

"That's one problem Leonard and I don't have."

Tim smiled. "No, you don't have to deal with that. It's pretty hard to landscape a yard remotely."

Lin noticed that Tim hadn't asked anything about the table and wondered about his disinterest. "I don't think you'll have any trouble with the table. It seems to have tapped itself quiet."

Tim blinked and then said, "Oh. Good. Was it a pain to have it at your house?"

"Not at all."

"Well, thanks. I hope it stays quiet."

"How are you doing?" Lin asked gently.

"I'm good." Tim took a swallow from his cup, and then he let out a long sigh. "I guess things aren't great. I'm struggling with feeling alone. It's a big house and I'm all by myself. I start to feel lonely." The man shrugged.

"My cousin's coming for dinner tonight. Why don't you join us?"

"Oh, I don't know. I have so much to do. Thanks, but can I take a raincheck?"

"Sure." Lin nodded. "I was wondering ... have you recently broken up with someone?"

"No, I haven't. I haven't been in a relationship for a long time."

"Why not? Too busy with work?"

"It's not that. I date. I just can't seem to find the right woman. Sometimes I think I'll never find who I'm looking for."

"Don't give up. She's out there." Lin smiled. "And she's probably looking for you."

Tim gave a quick nod.

Lin recalled Viv's theory that there could be an angry spirit in Tim's house interfering with the owner's happiness. "What was your grandfather like?"

Tim's face brightened. "He was a ball of energy. He was a lawyer, but he was also an artist. He painted, sculpted. He loved making art. He could be quiet and intense when he was working on a piece, but he was jovial and funny the rest of the time."

"How long did he live here?"

"Oh, let's see. About thirty years? He bought the house shortly before I was born."

"Then clearly, he was happy here," Lin observed.

"I'm sure of it. He loved this house. He loved the island."

"You told me you came to visit when you were little?"

Tim nodded. "We lived on the west coast so we couldn't come every year. When I was in high school, I didn't come much anymore. There was so much to do with sports and friends and everything. I think I only came three of four times while I was in college and grad school, and then when I started working, I didn't visit at all. I saw Granddad though. My parents moved to Boston and my grandfather would fly over to visit."

"How did you feel when you visited here when you were little?"

"Excited. I loved the beach. We had a lot of fun. I loved Granddad. I always felt happy and comfortable here. I loved this house."

"Do you still love it now you're the owner?" Lin asked.

"Yeah, I do." Tim nodded vigorously. "I just need to get out and meet people. I need to manage my time better. By evening, I'm exhausted."

"Did you feel the same way when you were living in Boston?"

Tim's forehead creased as he considered the question. "I guess not as much. I had friends and they always wanted to go out ... for dinner, to a pub, to a sporting event. They wouldn't let me say no."

"You need to find some people like that here," Lin joked.

"I know." Tim looked pensive for a few moments. "Something feels like it's missing here. It doesn't have to do with my friends. It's ... I don't know ... I don't know what it is, but it picks at me. I've never felt like this before." He looked sheepish. "I don't know why I'm telling you this. I can't articulate it very well."

"You might just need time to get used to your new life here," Lin said encouragingly. "The pieces will fall into place."

Tim's face dropped and he looked pained for a few seconds until he was able to shake it off. "I think so. You're right. It's a lot of change in a short time. I'll settle in eventually." The young man noticed Lin's horseshoe necklace. "That's a beautiful piece of jewelry."

Lin's hand went to her necklace. "Thank you. It's an antique. It belonged to one of my ancestors. My cousin found it hidden in the ell at the back of her house. She gave it to me."

"She didn't want it for herself?" Tim asked.

"She thought I should have it. From what we know, I'm a lot like our long ago ancestor."

"What a great connection to have to the past." Tim paused again and he had a faraway look on his face.

"It sounds like you and your grandfather had a great connection with each other," Lin said.

"We did. I had great fun with him. Sometimes, he'd set me up with the same art supplies he was working with and we'd paint together for a couple of hours. I felt very important." Tim puffed out his chest and smiled.

"Do you still paint?"

"Not for a very long time. I should pick it up again."

"This house is sure big enough," Lin pointed out. "You should be able to find a workshop somewhere in all this space."

"I should do that. Set up a studio in here. Get some art supplies. It sounds very appealing. Something to get me out of my business mindset and into something enjoyable and just for me. Don't get me wrong, I love my business, but it would be really nice to just sit and paint and let my mind relax."

"That's a great idea. I bet your grandfather would be really happy about it."

"Where can I find art supplies on the island?" Tim asked.

Lin told him about two places that sold art supplies.

"I'll go tomorrow to pick up some things, some sketchpads, an easel, paints, pencils, pastels. Thanks for talking about this stuff with me. I never would have thought to start painting and drawing again."

"I'm glad you got the idea to do it."

Tim lowered his voice. "Listen, what was going on with that table?"

Lin chose her words carefully. "There were a few things it had to get out of its system."

"Was it angry about something?" Tim asked warily.

"I don't think so. It just needed some attention," Lin was being intentionally vague.

"Should I do anything for it?"

"There's nothing to do. It will be fine."

"What started it up?" Tim looked directly at Lin. "Does it have something to do with a ghost?"

Lin didn't want Tim to get worked up or worried about the issue since the idea of ghosts made him uneasy. "It might have, but it's all good now. Nothing to be concerned about. I think the table won't jump or wiggle or tap anymore. You should have peace and quiet from now on." Her eyebrows raised with a new thought. "Have you ever considered renting out some of the rooms in the house?"

"I haven't, no."

"If you aren't opposed to it, you might want to give it some thought. You could make some money from the rentals and you wouldn't be living in an empty home. There would be people to talk with, cook with, eat with. And because the house is so big, you could get away from each other whenever you wanted."

"It would be nice to have someone around to talk to," Tim said, "and not always be cooped up by myself alone in the house. Maybe some short term rentals would be a good idea, although a long term renter might be better. I could get to know the person, not have someone new coming every few days."

Lin nodded. "Just don't bite off more than you can chew. Think about it before you jump in." The young woman finished her coffee. "I should get going. Are you sure you can't get away to have dinner with me and my cousin tonight?"

"I really shouldn't. I have to buckle down and get some work done. Maybe I can make dinner for you and your cousin sometime."

"That would be great."

Despite Tim seeming more upbeat than when she arrived, Lin couldn't shake off the sensation that something wasn't right.

But what was it?

15

Lin and Viv chopped vegetables for a stir-fry dinner and made some rice and a green salad. The door was open from the kitchen to the deck and a warm, pleasant breeze came in from outside. Nicky and Queenie were in the meadow behind the house having an adventure.

"There's something that feels off about Tim." Lin filled a wooden bowl with greens.

Viv stirred the rice into the pot of boiling water. "How do you mean? He's not sincere?"

"I think he's very sincere. What I feel about him is hard to describe. There seems to be something bothering him and he doesn't know what it is or he's unable to articulate it."

Viv said, "It's probably the move to the island

and the big change to his usual routine that's got him feeling off. People make changes and think everything will be smooth sailing, but they forget that change can be difficult even when it's a great thing or something you've always wanted. You need time to acclimate and transition to the new situation."

"I think you're right." Lin added onions and tomatoes to the salad. "Even when it's something you want or always dreamed of, you need time to get used to the change in your life. You expect you'll be thrilled and happy, and when you're not, you think something is wrong, but it's only because you're adjusting to a new normal."

"Tim does need to get out of that house," Viv said. "He needs people to interact with. He needs some fun, not just work, work, work all the time. What's the good of having lots of money if you have no one to enjoy it with?"

"I wouldn't know." Lin mixed ingredients for dressing. "But, I'd like to find out ... I mean the part about having lots of money, not the part about having no one to enjoy it with."

"Win the lottery, will you? Then you can see how great it is to share it with me." Viv added a little oil to the wok and heated it over the burner.

"Do you want to go to the museum library tomorrow after work and try to find information about the other owners of Tim's house? We can see if a lot of them met with misfortune. And if they did, we might want to talk to Libby about the possibility of an angry spirit living in Tim's new home."

Lin stirred some seasoning into the rice. "When I'm at the Colonial, I don't get the sense that a spirit is living there. I don't feel anyone's presence, good or bad."

"If you don't sense a ghost there, then my theory is probably incorrect," Viv said as she poured a little soy sauce into the wok. "It was a good idea though."

"It was." Lin became lost in her thoughts about what could be influencing Tim's sad mental state. "There are too many questions and not enough answers. What's bothering Tim, what does Ezra Cooper want? I know he told us he wants love, but what does that mean? I know I keep asking the same questions over and over."

"We'll have to keep asking them until we get answers." Viv scooped the wok meal into a bowl and after putting on sweaters, they carried the food outside to the deck.

The setting sun created strokes of pinks and

violets like someone had taken a paint brush and swept the colors across the sky.

Nicky and Queenie emerged from the field and plopped down on the patio to watch the birds flying overhead.

"Has Ezra shown up again?" Viv questioned.

"He hasn't." Lin spooned some rice onto her plate and placed some veggies over the top.

"I'm not surprised," Viv sighed. "These spirits have to be so difficult. If I ever become a ghost, remind me not to be so mysterious and secretive when I want something."

Lin chuckled. "I'll remember to tell you."

The cousins discussed what needed to be done for the wedding and Lin offered to talk to some flower suppliers she knew to finalize the bouquets and table centerpieces.

"The music's taken care of and I'm doing the wedding cakes," Viv said. "We've picked out our dresses, so that's all set. I'll look into having invitations printed. Then the four of us will have to talk about the actual ceremony ... where we'll have it, how it will be set up, the vows, the music we want, a justice of the peace."

Lin's eyes widened. "I'm glad you know what you're doing, otherwise I'd be completely overwhelmed." With a grin, she added, "Maybe we should elope."

"It would certainly cost less," Viv nodded.

"The guys would be fine with it. They're so easy-going about the plans."

"I think John would be disappointed," Viv said. "He likes to mark an occasion. He enjoys special celebrations."

"He's getting his wish then," Lin said with a smile, "too many plans have been made already to cancel the ceremony and reception. And anyway, I'm looking forward to the day."

"Me, too. I'm really glad the four of us get to do this together. It's going to be very special."

"Why don't the four of us get together for dinner tomorrow night and we can talk about the ceremony and how we want it to be?" Lin asked.

"Good idea. Let's try that new restaurant on Centre Street," Viv suggested.

After enjoying a chocolate mousse pie for dessert along with cups of tea, the cousins cleaned up and Viv, complaining about the need to get up early for work the next morning, lifted Queenie into her arms and headed for home.

Lin and Nicky sat in the living room with the gas stove going to ward off the night chill. After completing some anagrams and a difficult crossword puzzle, Lin placed the puzzle books on the coffee table and then yawned, stretched out on the sofa, and rested her head on a throw pillow. "I'm just going to rest my eyes for a few minutes," she told the dog. "Then I'll take care of some bills before we turn in for the night."

In a few minutes, the young woman was sound asleep.

Nicky let out a soft yip causing Lin to stir. Lying on her stomach and feeling disoriented, she rubbed at her eyes and glanced around the dark room realizing she'd fallen asleep on the couch.

"I thought I left the lamp on." Lin reached down to pat the dog just as freezing air swirled against her back. She sat bolt upright, scrambling to sit straight, her heart pounding fiercely and her eyes scanning the room looking for the source of the cold.

"Ezra?"

Lin startled when she saw a ghost sitting in the rocking chair in the corner of the room, but it wasn't Ezra. It was a woman with dark blond hair wearing a long, light blue dress with a high collar. Her hair was pulled up in a bun, with soft tendrils falling around her face and she looked to be in her mid-twenties. The woman rocked gently in the chair with her hands clasped together on her lap.

Nicky stared at the spirit, his tail thumping against the floor.

"Abigail?" Lin whispered.

The ghost made eye contact with Lin, her facial expression soft and kind.

"Can you hear what I'm saying?" Lin asked.

The edges of Abigail's mouth turned up in the slightest smile.

"Do you know where Ezra is?"

The smile vanished.

"I saw him a few days ago."

The ghost's eyes widened.

"I asked him what he needed. He told me *love*."

A glistening tear formed in the corner of the ghost's eye and the moon's light shined on it as it spilled over and slipped down Abigail's cheek.

Lin was afraid the spirit would leave so she started to talk. "You and Ezra were married for about two years. You lived in the big Colonial on Old Lane at the top of Main Street."

Abigail brushed at her cheek.

Lin said softly, "You fell ... in town."

The ghost moved forward slightly, reached around, and touched her back. Then she moved her hand and touched the back of her neck.

Lin's neck and back where the only places on her body that felt the icy cold. "You hurt your back? And your neck?"

Abigail turned away and looked out the window into the darkness of the night.

After a few moments passed, Nicky glanced up at Lin and then he turned his gaze back to the ghost.

"Were you behind me when I was walking home the other night?" Lin questioned. "Is that why I felt the cold against my back?"

Abigail slowly turned her head away from the window and looked at Lin, her eyes blinking slowly.

Lin asked the question she'd asked earlier. "Do you know where Ezra is?"

The ghost's lower lip trembled.

A terrible thought entered Lin's mind. "Do you know that Ezra died a year after you did?"

Abigail looked alarmed.

"It seems he couldn't live without you. Ezra took his own life."

The ghost leaned back against the rocker, a look of horror on her face.

"I'm sorry, Abigail. I think Ezra is looking for you. I think he's trying to find you."

Abigail's face crumpled. The atoms that made up her body flashed bright red, black, and then red again. The light she gave off was so bright that Lin almost had to look away.

Nicky whined. He seemed to want to rush to the spirit, but he held back.

Lin's heart contracted. She could almost feel the ghost's misery and loss, and her own eyes welled up. "Look for Ezra. Maybe you can find him."

Tears poured down Abigail's face and her atoms begin to spin so fast that they became a blur, then they sparked and flared ... and she was gone.

Lin slipped off the sofa onto the floor next to her dog and she wrapped her arms around him as her own tears tumbled from her eyes.

"Maybe I shouldn't have told her about Ezra. Did I do the wrong thing, Nick?"

16

"You didn't do the wrong thing," Libby tried to reassure Lin.

The women sat at the desktop computers and microfiche machines in the library of the historical museum looking up the former owners of Tim's Colonial. Although she had planned to join Libby and Lin, Viv had two employees call out sick so she had to stay at the store and was unable to help with the task.

Lin's thumb and forefinger rubbed at her horseshoe necklace. "Abigail looked so grief-stricken when I told her Ezra had died so soon after she had. I felt terrible. I don't think I should have told her. But why didn't she know?"

Libby said quietly, "We know quite a lot about

paranormal activity and we have many skills that prove to us that the spirit lives on, but much remains a mystery and we will probably never know the answers to our questions until we pass ourselves. Somehow, Abigail didn't know what became of her husband. Perhaps, because you told her, she'll be able to locate Ezra now and the two will be together again."

"I hope so." Despite her statement, Lin didn't think it would work out that way and her heart ached for the ghosts who had lost each other. "Why can't they find one another? Why is everything so hard?"

"Don't give up on them, Carolin." Libby gave the young woman a gentle pat on the back. "Let's focus on our work."

While Lin looked up the land records associated with Tim's house, Libby searched for the owners' names in the news or online looking for any misfortune that might have befallen them.

They were able to go back through one-hundred-twenty-five years of ownership, and despite finding two early deaths due to disease, a death from a car accident, and another death due to a plane crash, they found no evidence that the occupants or owners of the antique Colonial experienced more misfortune than the general population.

"It was a good theory Viv had," Libby acknowledged. "And it deserved to be looked into, but there isn't any proof to back it up."

"So there's no bad spirit living in the Colonial wreaking havoc with the people who live there," Lin said.

"It doesn't seem so." Libby turned to Lin. "What do you make of these ghosts? Is Ezra trying to get your help so he can find Abigail? Is that why he's made an appearance?"

"It makes sense. I guess when he discovered I was here on the island and could see ghosts, he caused trouble with that table to try and get me to the house," Lin speculated. "It worked. But what else can I do? Ezra showed up when Abigail wasn't around, and Abigail showed up when Ezra wasn't around. Will me telling Abigail about her husband's death be enough for them to find each other?"

"Is it that simple?" Libby questioned.

The women made eye contact and could tell they both shared the same feelings on the subject.

"I didn't think so," Libby sighed.

"What are we going to do?" Lin's voice held a tone of hopelessness.

"You've never failed a ghost yet." Libby spoke encouragingly. "And you won't now. It's just going to take more time, that's all. You'll figure it out. Be patient."

Lin went for a run later in the day to try and clear her head, but all she could think about was Ezra and Abigail and the predicament they were in. Images of Abigail and the look of misery on her face kept popping into her mind making Lin feel awful and sluggish.

Why can't I understand how to help?

Lin returned home, took Nicky for a walk, then showered and changed, all the while wishing one, or both, of the ghosts would make an appearance, but neither showed up.

When it was time to go to the restaurant, Lin walked into town to meet Jeff, Viv, and John for dinner on Centre Street.

Jeff was waiting outside and when he saw his fiancée, he hurried to greet her, wrapping her in a hug. Noticing her expression, he asked what was wrong and she gave him the condensed version of what had happened the previous night.

"I agree with Libby. You didn't do anything wrong. You had to tell Abigail."

"I guess so."

They walked inside to get a table for four, and in a few minutes, Viv joined them at the table by the windows.

"What a day. I'm exhausted. John's running late, but he'll be here soon. What's wrong with you?" she asked her cousin.

When she heard the tale, Viv's face nearly paled. "I'm glad I wasn't there. I would have passed out." Her expression changed to confusion. "How can one ghost not know someone is dead? Don't they communicate with each other?"

Lin shrugged. "I have no explanation."

"This is a puzzle," Viv reached for her wine glass. "And I thought *I* had a tough day."

"Let's have an evening free from ghost talk," Lin suggested. "I could use a break."

They ordered some appetizers to share until John arrived.

Jeff told them about a project he was working on with his friend, Kurt. "The house is about two hundred years old. It's in town. Someone recently purchased the place for just under three million dollars and the new owner is pumping tons of money into the renovation. The place is going to be beautiful when it's done. All the best finishes are being used. It's being restored to its former glory."

"I'd love to see it," Lin told him.

"Where do these people get their money?" Viv sighed. "And why don't they adopt me?"

Lin and Jeff chuckled just as John hurried over to the table, gave Viv a kiss, and took a seat.

"What a crazy day. I got three new listings and two possible ones, and I sold a house in Madaket." A wide smile crossed the young man's face. "I love my job."

"I hope you sell the new listings fast. We have to pay for the wedding," Viv said.

"No worries," John told her. "Maybe we should buy a new car."

"Really?" Viv looked surprised.

"I should have a nice car to impress my clients, show them how successful I am, inspire confidence in them that I can sell their houses. It's marketing." The waiter brought John a beer and after he took a swallow of it, his eyes widened. "Oh, I almost forgot. I have a possibility of another listing. Someone came into the office today looking for me. The man might be interested in selling his house." John paused for effect as he moved his eyes from Viv to Lin. "You know him. Guess who?"

The cousins looked blank.

John shook his head in mock disappointment at

their inability to come up with the answer. "Tim Pierce."

Lin leaned forward with wide eyes. "Tim Pierce?"

"He's selling his house?" Viv was incredulous, then she gave John a look of distrust. "No way. You're kidding us."

John held up his hand like he was taking an oath. "I swear."

"What did he say to you?" Lin was shocked by the news.

"He said he had a house he'd recently inherited. He thought he'd be able to work remotely, but it wasn't working out the way he hoped. He might return to the mainland to live in Boston. He hasn't made up his mind yet, but he might want me to come by and see the house someday so I can give him an idea of what the place would sell for."

"I can't believe this," Viv was almost fuming. "Tim is being rash. He needs time to see if living here will work out for him. He loves Nantucket. A house like that comes along once in a lifetime ... and that's if you're very, very fortunate. I think Tim's making a huge mistake."

"Well, don't tell him that," John said reaching for his beer glass. "I want the listing."

"I agree with Viv," Lin said. "I think he needs to

give himself some time. He's being hasty and impulsive."

"When are you working at Tim's again?" Viv asked her cousin.

"Tomorrow. Leonard's meeting me there bright and early."

"Then talk to Tim when you're there," Viv urged. "Ask him what the heck he's doing. Talk some sense into him."

"Wait, no," John told them. "Let the man make his own decision. He's free to sell if he wants to. Don't badger him."

Viv replied, "Tim has been feeling lonely and out-of-sorts. I worry that he's in a fragile mental and emotional state and could end up making the wrong choice. Lin and I don't want him to make a decision that he'll deeply regret in the future."

"I think it would be okay if you talk to Tim about it," Jeff said. "Ultimately, it's his house and he should sell it if he wants to, but it doesn't hurt to discuss it with him to make sure he's thought the whole thing through and won't be sorry about his decision."

"How did he seem when he talked to you today?" Lin asked John.

"How do you mean?"

"Did he seem nervous? Hurried? Depressed? Low energy?"

"I don't know him. I don't know what he's usually like."

"If you had to describe Tim and his interaction with you, what would you say about him?" Viv asked.

John's face screwed up in thought. "He was business-like, but friendly. He was well-spoken. He asked good questions about the selling process. He made it clear he was only thinking about selling the house and wasn't sure if he'd pursue it. He seemed like a nice guy."

"When are you supposed to go see the house?" Lin asked.

John said, "Tim hasn't made a decision yet. He said he wanted to think about it more, but that it wouldn't hurt to get an estimate from me. He said he'd call me in a couple of days."

Oh, no. Lin's heart sank.

17

The newly landscaped beds were taking shape behind Tim's house. The weeds had been pulled, the brush removed, the beds were marked out and edged, and soil had been added to build them up and provide a good foundation for the new plants.

Lin and Leonard had been doing the heavy work all morning and they were ready for a break so they headed to sit in the shade next to Nicky who was dozing in the grass under a tall Maple.

Lin had knocked on the front and back doors of the house hoping to be able to talk to Tim about his plans for the Colonial, but no one answered. She hoped he wasn't giving up on living on the island, but if he was determined to move back to the mainland, she would wish him well.

"Some people don't care for island living." Leonard drank from his water bottle. "It's too isolating for them. Tim must be one of them."

"You're right. A lot of people would never choose to have a home on an island. If the reason for Tim wanting to move is loneliness, I wish he'd stay for a few months and socialize with us. He could meet our friends and make more friends through them. In a little while, he'll have a group he can enjoy being with and can count on for help if he needs it." Lin poured some water from her bottle into a bowl for Nicky.

When Lin first saw Leonard that morning, she told him all about the visit from Abigail Cooper so when the man said, "I wonder why those two can't find each other?" she knew what he was talking about.

"Libby says we can't really know about the other side. We do know some things, but ninety-nine percent is hidden from us. She said we can offer help when it's something we're capable of, but otherwise we have to let things go. Libby said someday we'll all know about the spirit world, but not while we're here living on the earthly plane."

Leonard huffed at that. "Hopefully, *someday* doesn't come too soon."

Nicky walked over and climbed onto Leonard's lap and the man gently ran his hand over the dog's fur. "I guess Nick thinks he's a cat."

Reaching into her lunchbox, Lin removed a dog treat for Nicky and some homemade granola for her and her partner.

"So what are you going to do about Ezra and Abigail?"

Lin shrugged. "I have to wait and see what happens, and if I can do something to help them, I will. It's not a very good answer, but it's all I have."

"It's the right answer. Time will tell if you can be of help." Leonard moved the dog to the side and stood up. "I'll head off to the other clients now. Text me if you need anything, Coffin."

"I will. I might doze off here against the tree for a few minutes before I start putting in the plants."

Leonard said, "Just don't sit there until nightfall. You want me to call you when it gets dark to make sure you're not still here?"

Lin chuckled. "Nicky will wake me up if I sleep too long."

"Keep an eye on her," Leonard told the dog before leaving the yard for his truck and heading off down the street to the next job.

The sun was shining and the air temperature

was pleasingly warm. Lin's muscles felt achy from all the heavy work she'd done that morning, so she closed her eyes to rest for a few minutes with Nicky on the grass beside her.

The image of a small, outside wedding on a perfect spring day drifted into her mind. A group of about forty guests sat in chairs on both sides of an aisle down which a minister led the bride and groom, dressed in their best clothes, followed by the couple's parents, and the bridesmaids and groomsmen.

The father of the bride hugged his daughter and shook hands with the groom, vows were exchanged as the happy couple held hands and beamed at one another, a ring was placed on the bride's finger, and the new husband and wife shared a brief, sweet kiss to the applause of the guests. After the ceremony and before leaving for the reception at the bride's father's home, the guests mingled and chatted and hugged the smiling couple, offering them heartfelt wishes.

Someone spoke Lin's name and her eyes opened and she scrambled to her feet. "Oh, hi. I was taking a rest."

"The yard is looking great." Tim stood before her

gazing around at the landscaping work she and Leonard had accomplished that morning.

"We knocked on the door when we got here, but I guess you were out."

"I had some errands to do."

"How's everything going?" Lin hoped Tim would tell her what he was thinking as far as putting the house on the market.

"The same." The man forced a smile. "I met a friend of yours the other day."

"John? He mentioned he spoke with you. Are you interested in selling?"

"He's a nice guy and from what I've read, he's a first-rate Realtor." Tim bent to pat Nicky. "You're a good dog." When the young man straightened, he said, "I don't know what's wrong. Being here is making me unbearably sad, but I have no idea why. I'm going to go back to Boston for a while."

Lin nodded. "Maybe that's for the best."

When the air around Lin turned wintry cold and the ghost of Sebastian Coffin appeared standing behind Tim's shoulder, she had to be careful to keep her face neutral all the while wondering why the spirit suddenly materialized.

"Maybe a week back in Boston will make you feel better," Lin told him.

Tim ran his hand over his cheek. "I was thinking I'd stay more than a week. I might make it permanent."

Lin's heart skipped a beat when she heard this news. She took a quick look at Sebastian. "Really? Do you think you might like to go back and forth between the island and the city? Have homes in both places for a while?"

"I don't know. All I know is I need to get away. I feel like I'm longing for something, but I just don't know what it is." Tim's forehead was lined with concern.

"A longing? Like you're missing something?" Lin asked.

"It's confusing. I'm having a hard time concentrating here. I feel off, restless. Yeah, I guess you could put it that way, that I'm missing something. I've got a business to run. I can't be flailing around trying to get my bearings, trying to feel settled." Tim looked at Lin. "Do you want to come in and have a cold drink?"

"Sure." Lin nodded. "That would be great."

Lin and Nicky went into Tim's kitchen where he fumbled around in the refrigerator. "I've got iced tea, some seltzer, juice, beer."

"Iced tea, please."

Sebastian stayed right behind the man as he moved around the kitchen. Lin absent-mindedly reached for her horseshoe necklace.

Tim poured the tea into tall glasses and handed one to Lin. Before taking a seat at the island with his guest, he took out some plain biscuits from the cabinet and gave one to the dog.

"I love the island, but I can't seem to settle in." Tim took a long drink from his glass. "I feel antsy all the time. I'm not sleeping well."

"Have you had sleep problems in the past?" Lin asked.

"Once in a while, but not like this. I have trouble falling asleep and I have trouble staying asleep. It's driving me nuts."

"Maybe you should see your doctor," Lin suggested. "There are all kinds of minor things that can interfere with getting a good night's sleep."

"I will." Tim nodded. "I thought about that, too."

"Are you definitely putting the house on the market?"

"No, not definitely. I want John to take a look at the house and let me know what he'd suggest listing it for," Tim said. "I'll spend some time in Boston and think everything over."

"You have a good plan."

Sebastian made eye contact with Lin and shook his head.

"Or maybe you could stay a little longer here and see if things get better."

The ghost nodded.

"I'll see how things go."

Lin didn't think Tim had any intention of seeing how things went and she couldn't understand why Sebastian wanted the young man to stay on-island. She gave the ghost a quick look of exasperation. "I should get back to work. Thanks for the drink. I hope you stay."

"Thanks, Lin."

Lin and Nicky returned to the yard where Sebastian was already waiting for them.

Lin picked up an iron rake and pretended to be smoothing out the soil in one of the beds in case Tim looked out the window.

Looking at her ancestor, she asked, "Why don't you want Tim to leave?"

Sebastian adjusted the collar of his eighteenth-century shirt and stared at Lin.

Letting out a sigh, Lin asked, "I can't force him to stay. I've tried to talk him into giving it more time, but he's sad and uneasy living here. I've tried to find information about the house. There's nothing wrong with the place as far as our research has told us. What can I do?"

Sebastian stared into his descendant's eyes for several long moments and Lin could feel something stirring in her mind ... wisps of sounds ... a whisper of a word.

Make him stay.

Lin opened her mouth to speak as the particles that made up the ghost began to spin and flash, and then Sebastian was gone.

"Wait!" Lin called, but it was too late. The ghost was no longer standing before her.

"How can I make Tim stay?" Lin asked the dog. "I can't tie him up and throw him in the basement. It's easy to tell me to make him stay here. What I need to know is how to do it."

18

It was the day of the Nantucket Historical Museum garden party fundraiser and the event was being held in the garden of one of the old sea captain's houses on Main Street. The beautiful, white three-story Colonial with black shutters was built in the 1790s and was located on the upper part of Main Street a short distance from the stores and restaurants in the hub of town.

The original settlement of Nantucket, called Sherburne, dated back to 1673, and the cobblestones in the street had been installed around 1837 to keep mud from forming on the road. The lovely, tree-shaded Main Street was lined with Greek Revival mansions and seafarers' Colonials.

John and Jeff couldn't make the early evening

garden party so Lin and Viv went alone wearing their prettiest spring dresses.

The rear yard of the house was decorated with strings of white lights strung overhead, music played, floral arrangements had been placed around the garden, and waiters served cocktails and hors d'oeuvres on silver trays. Men in suits and women in spring dresses mingled with each other and enjoyed the music.

As the cousins sipped drinks and strolled around the gardens, someone called to them.

Leonard's girlfriend, Heather, and her niece, Lori, and a few other women walked over to greet Lin and Viv. Heather introduced everyone to each other and the small group stood on the stone patio by a water feature chatting about the gardens.

Lori's straight, dark blond hair tumbled over the shoulders of her short-sleeved, violet-colored dress. "What a fabulous garden this is. Heather told me there's a house and garden tour in August. I can't wait for it. I'm going to buy a ticket as soon as they go on sale."

"We love the annual garden party," Viv told her. "We come every year and we try to make the house tour, too." With a smile, Viv said, "Maybe when you go on the house tour, you'll find the house from your dreams."

Lori gave a nod and a smile that seemed somewhat forced to Lin. When Viv became engrossed in conversation with two other women, Lori moved a little closer to Lin.

"I've been having that house dream every night," she confided. "Sometimes more than once a night. I wake up disoriented and can't fall back to sleep."

"Have they become more frequent?" Lin asked.

"They sure have. Ever since coming to the island to work with Heather, a night doesn't go by without me dreaming about that house." Lori pressed a finger against her temple. "When I bring it up with Heather, she just chuckles and brushes it off. She thinks I'm being silly so I don't talk to her about it anymore. I swear I know that house and it means something important to me." Lori made eye contact with Lin. "You must think I'm nuts."

"Not at all. Why do you think your dreams are happening more often?" Lin wanted to know if Lori had a theory.

"I have no idea. I love the dream when it's going on, but it's making me feel exhausted the next day." Lori sipped from her glass.

"It could be happening more frequently because you moved to a place where you've always been excited to live," Lin speculated. "Maybe the dreams will slow down after the newness of living here wears off."

"That makes a lot of sense. That must be why I'm dreaming about the house so much." Lori looked wistfully around at the gardens. "I wish I could find it. Maybe it doesn't even exist. I always wonder if I was in it once as a child. Maybe the house has nothing to do with Nantucket. It may very well be somewhere else I went when I was very little."

"That's certainly possible," Lin said. "I bet you'll find it one day."

Lori smiled. "That would be my lucky day. Then maybe my dreams will stop and I won't be so tired the next morning. I wish I knew what the outside of the house looked like. I could drive around and look for it."

"Try thinking about wanting to see the outside of the place before you fall asleep," Lin suggested. "The memory of it could be buried deep in your subconscious. The image of the outside of the home might bubble up into your mind."

Lori tilted her head slightly to the side. "You take me seriously."

"Sure, I do," Lin chuckled.

"Well, most people don't. They think I'm making too much of a silly dream."

"Dreams aren't silly," Lin said. "They can tell us a lot about what's going on in our lives ... if we listen to them. They help us process things that happened during the day. They help us store memories. Some researchers think dreams help us solve problems, make connections, help us be more creative, help us process our emotions."

"So why am I always dreaming about this house? What does it mean?"

"I'm not an interpreter." Lin shrugged. "But on the surface, it seems like the house makes you feel safe. It's a place where you feel loved, appreciated, peaceful."

"All those things, yes." Lori nodded.

"It's a lovely place to go after a busy or stressful day. It's a retreat for your heart and soul. It's a place where you belong," Lin told her. "Everyone would love a place like that."

Lori's eyes teared up, but she blinked them away. "You describe it so perfectly. That's exactly how I feel in the dream." She brushed at her eyes and laughed. "I *need* to find that house."

Lin chuckled. "Well, when you find it, don't forget to invite me over."

Viv and Lin sat at a small table at the edge of the garden enjoying scones, strawberries, and whipped cream.

Viv licked her fork. "Yum. I'm in heaven."

Lin gave her cousin a little kick under the table. "Licking your fork in public is rude. If anyone sees you, we'll be banned from coming next year."

Viv lifted another bite of the scone to her lips. "This dessert is so good I forgot my manners."

"I guess that's a solid defense," Lin laughed. "The organizers of the garden party will forgive your lapse in good behavior."

Libby Hartnett, wearing an ankle-length, cream-colored dress and matching long sweater, came by and sat down at the cousins' table. "This event is packed. In the future, they're going to have to split the evening into two nights to accommodate all the people who want to attend."

"I didn't even know you were here," Lin said. "I didn't see you in the crowd."

"That's what I mean. It's becoming much too crowded to be enjoyable. Two evenings with a manageable amount of guests would be much better." Libby set down her drink and looked pointedly at Lin. "What's going on. Is anything new?"

Lin told Libby that Tim Pierce might be planning to sell the Colonial.

"That would be a shame," Libby said.

"And this morning I saw Sebastian at Tim's house when I was there. He spoke to my mind. He wants me to stop Tim from leaving the island."

Libby's eyes grew wide. "Did Sebastian suggest how you might go about forcing the man to stay?"

"No, he did not."

Leaning back in her chair, the older woman let out a sigh. "Why does Sebastian want Tim to stay here so badly?"

Viv leaned forward. "This is one of my chief complaints ... about ghosts, not in general. If Sebastian is so determined to have Tim remain here, couldn't he give Lin some help with how to get him to stay?"

"We must deal with the cards we are given, Vivian," Libby told her. "Complaining about it won't help."

Viv sipped from her drink. "Somehow, complaining *does* help *me*."

"I have a friend visiting from the mainland soon." Libby addressed the information to Lin. "She might prove helpful to you. When she arrives, I'll have you meet her. She knows a few things about ghosts."

"Okay, good. We can use all the help we can get." Lin nodded.

"Have you seen Ezra or Abigail again?" Libby asked.

"I haven't. They've gone quiet," Lin said.

Libby tapped her chin with her index finger. "They'll be back. Or one of them will, at least."

"Maybe they found each other," Viv said hopefully.

"If they did, they would have shown themselves to Lin so she'd know they were together," Libby explained. "They're still apart. I'm sure of it."

Lin fiddled with the end of a strand of her hair. "For some reason, I have a funny feeling."

"Funny how?" Viv asked suspiciously.

"Like time is running out." Lin's face was serious. "Like if Ezra and Abigail don't find each other soon, it will be too late for them."

Viv's expression changed to one of alarm. "Oh, no. How much time do they have left?"

"I don't know, but I don't think it's very long. A week?"

"This is terrible," Viv worried. "Can you get that tapping table back and tell them to hurry up?"

"I don't think that will help." Lin looked down at her empty dessert plate.

"What will help?" Viv questioned.

"I don't know." Lin shrugged helplessly. "I'm good for nothing on this case." A chill washed over Lin and as she rubbed her hand on her arms to rid them of goosebumps, she saw the shimmering ghost of Emily Witchard Coffin standing in the middle of the garden at the back of the yard.

"Don't sell yourself short, Carolin," Libby said. "You mustn't give up. You know more than you think, and you'll discover what you need to do in time to help the ghosts." The woman put her hand over Lin's. "We're lucky to have you here with us."

Emily nodded and smiled sweetly at Lin.

19

Lin and John met in front of Tim's Colonial home.

When John took out a key as they walked down the brick walkway to the front door, Lin asked, "Why do you have a key? Where's Tim?"

"Tim flew back to Boston today."

Lin almost jumped out of her skin. "What? He's gone?"

"Only for the day. He'll be back late tonight. He gave me the key so I could look around the house while he's gone." John pushed open the door and they entered into the foyer.

The wood floor gleamed and a pewter and crystal chandelier hanging from the high ceiling sparkled its light onto the entryway. An antique side table stood on the left wall with a painting of a sailing ship positioned over it. The carved wooden staircase stood to the right and there were two sitting rooms on each side of the foyer.

"It's a beautiful entryway." Lin admired the details on the staircase. "It's a grand welcome to the home."

"You sound like a Realtor." John wrote some notes on his tablet before walking into the sitting room on the left.

A fireplace graced one wall and a rug in soft shades of green, blue, and rose covered the floor. The high ceilings gave the room an elegant, spacious feeling. The room to the right of the foyer was similar in layout and furnishings, and Lin noticed that the tilt table had been placed against the wall near the windows.

When she walked over and gently placed her hand on the table, she couldn't feel any energy coming off of it. Everything about it was calm. She couldn't sense any ghostly activity near the piece of furniture.

Lin and John walked past a library and a dining room before entering the huge kitchen.

"This is going to be a big selling feature," John said. "The cabinetry was done by a well-known company and they must have cost an arm and a leg.

The granite is top-notch, the wood floors look great, the kitchen island is enormous, and take a look at the breakfast space. Those floor-to-ceiling windows bring in a ton of natural light. People are going to go nuts for this house. I bet it will sell fast once it's listed."

Lin groaned. "Don't entice Tim into selling with a statement like that."

"Why do you care if Tim sells this house and leaves the island?" John asked as he made some notes about the kitchen and took some pictures with his phone. "You barely know him."

Lin was about to speak, but she closed her mouth when she realized she didn't have a good answer. *Why do I care if he leaves?*

She thought about the mental message Sebastian sent her about not letting Tim leave the island.

Why does Tim need to stay? Lin stood still as her heart began to race. *Is Tim important to Ezra and Abigail being able to find each other? But how? What would he need to do to enable the ghosts to meet again?*

Lin's mind was racing from one improbable possibility to another. *This used to be Ezra and Abigail's home. Is there some way to get both ghosts back here at the same time? Why would that require Tim to stay on Nantucket?*

"I don't know why I'd like Tim to stay," Lin admitted. "He's a nice guy and it would be a shame for him to part with this house, but maybe that has nothing to do with anything. Maybe he has to be here to help the ghosts. Maybe Ezra and Abigail could find one another here, but I don't know what role Tim would play in bringing them back together. All I know is Sebastian told me not to let Tim leave."

"That might be hard." John led the way to the solarium. "You can't lock him in the basement until who knows when. Why not just tell him the reason? Those two ghosts need him around so they can get back together."

"I don't know if that *is* the reason he's supposed to stay." Lin was beginning to feel uneasy being in the house. She kept expecting a ghost to make an appearance in one of the rooms and she felt on edge and nervous.

"You'd think a couple of ghosts would be able to find each other in the spirit world," John said snapping some photos of the solarium.

"We don't know how it works," Lin explained. "If we did, we'd be better at helping."

"Let's go up to the bedrooms. Tim told me there are seven of them." John and Lin climbed the staircase and walked from room to room.

Every once in a while, Lin felt cool air around her, but no one materialized. When she entered the master bedroom, a wave of sadness engulfed her as she moved about the room. She began to suspect the chill was the effect of leftover currents moving through the space from long, long ago ... the sensation of many lives that had moved through these rooms. The sadness she picked up on was most likely from the terrible grief that Ezra had left behind hundreds of years ago. She was amazed that those emotions could still be floating on the air.

"Is being in the house helping you?" John asked.

"I don't know. I feel things while I'm walking around, but I don't know if it will lead me to anything." Lin gave a shrug.

A room Tim was using as an office was in the middle of the second floor and when John and Lin entered the space, a cold, energizing wave hit her like a ton of bricks and she had to take a step back. Glancing quickly around the office, she looked for something that might have caused the strange feeling. Her skin felt like pins and needles were pricking at her. Nothing seemed out of the ordinary. Everything looked normal. Lin wondered if Tim might experience feelings similar to hers while he worked in the room.

"This place is fabulous," John said as they headed down to the first floor. "Some beautiful updates have been done, but the work has been faithful and respectful to the home and its history."

Descending the stairs, Lin kept having the urge to look back over her shoulder at the office room located on the second floor. The impulse to return to the office was almost overwhelming.

"Do you feel anything when you're walking around in here?" Lin asked John.

John's face took on a look of shock. "Feel anything? Like what?" He looked warily around the hallway and into the rooms they were passing.

Lin wanted to chuckle at John's reaction. "You know," she teased, "ghosts, the sensation of something or someone walking close to you, a feeling of nervousness, a sense of dread."

"Stop it," John ordered, picking up his pace to hurry to the kitchen. "You're freaking me out."

When they reached the kitchen and John turned to face Lin, there were beads of perspiration on his forehead. "You love scaring me, don't you? You know I hate that kind of stuff. I'm not going to pretend to be tough. It scares me to death." John looked around the bright kitchen. "Did you see something? Should we be worried? Why don't we get out of here? We can come back another time."

"I sense things in the house, but they're nothing you need to be concerned about." Lin felt badly about frightening John and tried to reassure him. "I'm sorry I scared you. Nothing's going to happen. We're safe here."

"Are you sure? How do you know?" John quickly gathered up some papers from the kitchen island.

Lin reminded him, "I have some experience with ghosts."

"Whatever. Let's get out of here. I'm done for now. We can come back another time."

As they were leaving the house, Lin asked, "What's the date today? Is it the tenth?"

"It's the eleventh." John pulled the front door shut and locked it.

Lin thanked John for including her in his walk-through of the house and apologized again for teasing him.

"Maybe I won't take you along next time I come." John opened the car door and put his briefcase inside.

"Maybe by then you'll forget that I teased you," Lin smiled.

"Don't count on it." John gave Lin a mock mean look and she knew he wasn't angry with her.

After parting ways, Lin made a detour into town and then drove her truck to make one more stop before heading home.

Lin pulled close to the side of the road and got out, flicking on her flashlight and walking along the path into the Old North Cemetery. Despite the darkness, she found the graves she was looking for and placed the bouquet of flowers she'd brought next to the headstone in a little pool of moonlight.

"Happy Anniversary to both of you," Lin whispered. "It's been a little over two hundred and forty years since your wedding day. Isn't that amazing? But I guess time doesn't really have any meaning for you anymore." She sank down and sat on the damp ground. "I know you still love each other and I'm still trying to figure out how to bring you both together again. I promise I won't give up." She let out a long sigh. "Don't you give up either."

20

"Lin was mean to me." John set the platter of appetizers on the table. "I'm never inviting her along to see a house with me ever again."

The daylight was fading as Lin, Jeff, Viv, and John sat around the table of John's boat at the Nantucket town docks. Couples and families enjoying the evening weather strolled past on the docks to look at the boats.

"Just pretend there's no such thing as ghosts." Viv tried to keep a straight face. "If you can't see them, then they mustn't exist."

"It's worse if I know they exist and I can't see them." John passed around a bottle of wine. "How do I know if they're creeping up behind me?" He had to look over his shoulder to be sure nothing ghostly stood behind him.

Jeff said, "I don't think we have to worry. The ghosts know we're good for nothing so they won't bother us."

"I won't tease you anymore." Lin scooped some cheesy nachos onto her plate. "Or will I?" she added slyly.

"Did you learn anything about the house?" Viv asked. "Anything that might help bring Ezra and Abigail together?"

"There's a room on the second floor that Tim is using as an office," Lin told the group. "I was hit with strange feelings when I stepped into that room."

"What sort of feelings?" Jeff questioned.

"My skin felt all prickly." Lin had to rub her arms remembering the sensation. "The room felt cool, but not cold enough to indicate a ghost was about to appear. It was more like traces of spirits moving around the space from the people who once lived there."

John groaned at the comment. "I don't think I'll be going back to that room when I return to the house to take measurements and better pictures."

"Why do you feel those traces of past lives only in that room?" Viv sipped from her wine glass.

Lin gave a shrug. "I don't know, but the feeling is powerful. I'd like to go back there ... if John will let me go with him again."

"Don't count on it," John muttered. "Maybe if I go in daylight, you can come along."

"Have you given any more thought to why Sebastian wants you to try and convince Tim to stay on-island?" Jeff asked.

"I've given it a lot of thought." Lin wiped her fingers on a napkin. "There's only one thing I can come up with. Could Tim be a descendant of Ezra and Abigail?"

The others were silent for a few moments.

Viv asked, "That's an interesting idea, but why would that matter?"

"All I can think of is ... that Tim, being a descendant, can somehow act as a conduit to bring the ghosts together. Plus, he's living in the same house where Ezra and Abigail once lived."

"That actually makes a lot of sense," Jeff nodded.

"What does Tim have to do to get the ghosts together?" John asked.

"I don't know," Lin said disappointedly.

Viv perked up. "You said you felt odd when you were in the room Tim uses as an office. Could that room be important to the ghosts finding each other?"

Lin's eyes brightened. "I wonder." She looked to John. "When are you going back to Tim's house?"

"Not until Tim wants to go ahead and sell. Then I'll go back to take better pictures and do measurements for the listing. If Tim decides not to sell, then I won't be going back."

"Has he given you any idea which way he might be leaning?" Viv asked.

"Not really. I only spoke with him briefly since he returned from Boston the other night."

"I'd really like to get back into that room on the second floor," Lin told them.

"If I get the go-ahead, I'll let you know," John said and then he gave Lin a narrowed-eyed look. "But no more scaring me with ghost-talk when we're in there."

Lin smiled. "I promise."

Lin's phone buzzed in her sweater pocket and when she saw the text, her heart jumped into her mouth. "It's Tim."

"What does he want?" Viv's expression had turned wary when she saw her cousin's face tighten.

"The table is tapping again. He says it's out of control. He wants us to come as soon as we can."

The Haunted Past

Lin's eyes looked to her three companions around the small table.

"Go," Jeff urged. "Shall we come with you?"

"Not me," John said. "No, thanks. I'll come if you need me, but I won't be any good to you."

"It's okay," Lin told John as she stood up. "You can stay here. Thanks for offering though."

"I'll go with you," Viv said.

"Me, too," Jeff nodded.

"I'll keep the drinks cold for when you return." John stood to clear away the dishes. "We can have pizza when you get back. No worries. Good luck."

The threesome left the boat, hurried along the docks, and practically ran up Main Street.

When they arrived at Tim's house, the man was standing on the front step waiting for them. His face was pale and his facial muscles sagged. "I'm sorry to bother you, but that table is driving me nuts. It's jumping and banging and I can't take it. I don't know what to do with it. Will you take it away? I can't have it in the house. Keep it. I don't want it returned."

"When did it start?" Lin asked.

"As soon as I got back from my trip to Boston. It was late, I was exhausted, and then it started up. I yelled at it and it stopped. It was quiet for twenty-four hours and then an hour ago it all started again. I told it to stop, but it won't. I don't understand how this can be happening." Tim rubbed at the side of his face. "Why is it doing this? *How* is it doing this?"

"Why don't we have a look?" Lin suggested and Tim opened the door to allow them in.

"I'm staying out here. It's in the sitting room to the right." Tim sat down on the top step to wait.

Lin, Viv, and Jeff slowly walked inside and saw the table in its spot by the wall.

When Lin touched it, the table began to jiggle. It leaned slightly this way and that, the legs rhythmically tapping against the wood floor.

"I've never seen anything like it." Jeff's eyes were wide, but he didn't seem disturbed by what was happening.

"I'd like never to see anything like it again," Viv whispered and moved a little behind Jeff. "What does it want?"

"Let's take it back to my house." As soon as Lin said the words, the table stopped and went quiet.

Jeff picked it up and carried it outside.

"It stopped?" Tim asked looking at the table like it was a rattlesnake ready to strike.

"It went quiet," Lin said. "I'll take it home for now."

"You can keep it," Tim was adamant. "I'll drive you home."

The four people and the table rode in Tim's Jeep to Lin's cottage.

"I don't care what you do with it." Tim leaned out the window. "If you don't want it, give it away."

Jeff carried the table inside and set it down in the kitchen, staring at it.

Nicky greeted the people and sniffed at the table wagging his little tail.

"Will it start up anytime it wants to?" Jeff asked.

"Pretty much," Lin said.

Jeff eyed the table waiting to see if it would begin its tapping. "What does it want?"

"The age-old question," Viv sighed. "Shall I get the pen and paper from the drawer?"

Lin nodded. "Will you help me?" she asked her fiancé.

"You know I will. What should I do?"

Lin explained the process and she and Jeff sat in chairs pulled close to the table. Viv sat at the island ready to transcribe the taps.

Taking in a long, deep breath, Lin spoke. "Is it you, Ezra? Do you have something to tell us?"

Jeff made eye contact with Lin and she nodded reassuringly. After five minutes passed, the table rose an inch off the floor and for a moment, Jeff looked like he might flee the room.

"It's okay," Lin softly said. "This is what it does."

The tapping began. Five taps, pause. Twenty-six taps, pause. The sequence continued with taps and pauses until the table seemed to sputter.

All the legs tapped the ground at the same time, then it hovered in the air an inch over the floor, before the legs simultaneously tapped again. The sputtering went on for almost a full minute, and then the table set down on the floor with a mighty bang.

Breathing fast with near-disbelief, Jeff removed his hands from the tabletop. "What did it tell us?"

Viv cleared her throat. "The first word spelled was *Ezra*. The second word spelled was *Abigail*. The last word was *Tim*. The table seemed to want to tell us something else, but it rattled like it ran out of energy."

"Why the three names together?" Lin looked deep in thought.

"What else did it want to say before it ran out of gas?" Viv asked.

"I bet it was important," Lin told them with a drawn-out sigh. "Whatever the table was going to spell would have tied everything together."

Nicky woofed, his tail still wagging.

"Maybe we can try again later," Viv suggested.

"I don't think it will work later." Lin ran her hand over the top of the table. "Ezra seems to need at least a few days, maybe a week, before he can communicate again."

Viv groaned. "I hope that won't be too late."

21

Lin and Nicky arrived at Anton Wilson's house early in the morning before heading off to the landscaping job. Lin sat next to Anton at the kitchen table eating waffles with fresh fruit and the dog sat by the screen door looking out into the yard.

Anton pulled over his laptop so they could look at his notes while they were eating. "After you called last night, I did a few hours of research on the question." The historian pointed to the screen at an ancestral family tree. Tim Pierce is not descended from Ezra and Abigail Cooper. He is not even remotely related to either one of the Coopers."

Lin deflated. She hoped Tim might be a link to the ghosts. "That's disappointing."

"I know it's not the answer you were hoping for,

but at least knowing Tim isn't a relative of your ghosts, you won't go off in the wrong direction," Anton offered. "It's narrowing down the information so you'll be able to find the solution to how to get the ghosts back together."

Lin let out a sigh. "I was sure I was on to something."

"Keep looking. You'll find the answer." Anton went to the counter and returned with the coffee pot. "Another cup?"

"Half, please," Lin said. "Is Tim related to anyone who used to live on Nantucket?"

"Only his grandfather who recently passed away. Otherwise, Tim's roots are in the Northeast, and then his ancestors go back to Canada, and then to France and England. There's nothing that points to a previous Nantucket connection."

"Okay," Lin said more to herself than to Anton. "So familial lines aren't what will bring Ezra and Abigail back together." She took a sip of the coffee. "I'm stumped." She relayed what happened with the table the previous night.

A look of amazement washed over Anton's face. "Jeff was there?"

Lin gave a nod. "He handled the whole thing really well."

"He's a strong man." Anton appeared glad he himself hadn't witnessed the table tapping episode. "So the table tapped out three names? Ezra, Abigail, and Tim? It had something else to say before it stopped?"

"It tried to give us more information, but it couldn't do it. If only it could have kept going." An expression of disappointment showed on Lin's face. "I think we were so close to understanding what to do. I don't think we'll get any new information for a week. Ezra seems to lose the ability to communicate through the table after a few minutes of the tapping, and then he needs to recharge for six or seven days." She finished the last of her waffle and strawberries. "Ezra and Abigail had their wedding anniversary the other day."

"Is what's going on with the ghosts a result of the anniversary?" Anton asked.

"The couple was married in the month of May, Abigail died in the month of April, and Ezra died at the end of May in the year following his wife's death. The spring of different years was both a happy time and an incredibly sad time for them. But it's been centuries since they lived and died. Why are the ghosts appearing now?"

"Well, we've said it might be because they know

you can see them," Anton reminded Lin. "Perhaps, no one with your abilities has been known to them before now."

"I think that's part of it, but there has to be a more pressing reason." Lin rested her chin in her hand and leaned on the table. "There has to be something that's happening on the island right now that's bringing Ezra and Abigail forward."

"And what does Tim Pierce have to do with it?" Anton asked.

Lin shook her head slowly from side to side.

Nicky whined and turned around to look at the humans.

"We had the Daffodil Festival and the annual garden party fundraiser for the historical museum," Lin thought out loud. "But neither of those things are new this year so they're not the reason the ghosts are suddenly making contact."

"Tim is new this year," Anton pointed out. "He recently moved here."

Lin cocked her head to the side considering. "That's true. Is there some link from him to the ghosts? If there is, what could it be? Tim had been here in his grandfather's Colonial house when he was little, but that doesn't connect him to Ezra and

Abigail. He's not a descendant of theirs. So what's left?"

"I have some time later today," Anton told her. "I'll do some more digging. I'll look for a possible link."

Lin reached over and gave the man a hug. "You know when I first moved back here, I thought you and Libby might be bad people. I even had the thought you might be trying to kill me."

"For heaven's sake, Carolin. How in the world did you ever think such a thing? Why didn't you ever tell me?"

"I thought you knew. I think I did tell you."

"Well, I must have blocked it out. Kill you? Honestly. I know you can be very annoying, but...."

Lin made a face and narrowed her eyes at the historian.

"I'm kidding," Anton said and then he tapped his finger against his chin. "Or am I?"

~

Lin and Nicky were working in Tim Pierce's yard when the young man came out of the house to talk.

"What happened with that table?"

"It's gone quiet again," Lin told him.

"Why was it having a fit?"

Since Tim found the idea of ghosts unsettling, Lin didn't want to burden him with the details. "It has something to do with spirits."

"Is it haunted?"

"No. It just has a need every now and then to act up." She smiled. "It's harmless."

Tim scratched the side of his head trying to understand, but thought it best to let it be.

Lin wanted to change the subject. "Did you have a good trip to Boston?"

"It was a busy day, but I got a lot done." Tim glanced at the back of the house. "It's a beautiful place, isn't it?"

"It certainly is," Lin agreed.

"I don't think I can stay here." Tim kicked at a pebble in the grass.

Lin waited for him to say more.

"I'm lonely here." Tim looked at the young woman beside him. "I love this house. I love the island. But there's something about this place that makes me inconsolably sad and lonely."

"Do you feel that way anywhere else?" Lin asked.

"I don't. Only here. Only in this house." Tim looked down at the ground and shook his head.

Lin took a chance and asked, "Have you ever heard of Ezra and Abigail Cooper?"

Tim's head popped up. "They sound familiar. Who are they?"

"They used to own this house," Lin said.

"How long ago?"

"Centuries ago."

Tim's eyebrow went up. "Why do you mention them?"

"They were only married a short time. Only two years. Abigail died in an accident. It seems she fell when she was in town and hit her head. Ezra was inconsolable." Lin used the same word Tim had used about himself to describe Ezra's grief.

Tim's eyes watered and he swallowed hard to clear his throat. "That's terrible."

"Does the story sound familiar? Had you heard about them before?"

"No." Tim looked again at the back of his house. "Is it possible that the man's grief over his wife lingers in the house? Is that the reason I feel so sad when I'm here?"

"Maybe. I can sometimes feel emotions floating on the air. I don't know if what you're feeling is tied to the sad story of the couple."

"I really don't want to leave," Tim admitted.

"Then stay," Lin said gently.

"I don't know if I can. I had John take a quick look at the house." Tim straightened his posture. "I'm torn about what I should do. I don't know if I'll ever find what I want if I stay here. I want ... I want a happy life. I want a wife, someone to love, a family, people to share my life with."

"You don't think you can make a life like that here?" Lin asked.

"I don't know." Tim ran his hand over his face. "There's just too much sadness in this house."

Cold air wrapped itself around Lin and when she looked up, Sebastian and Emily Witchard Coffin stood shimmery and translucent right behind Tim.

The ghosts were holding hands and Emily reached her free hand out as if she wanted to grasp Tim on the shoulder to offer some comfort, but her fingers hovered in the air like a whisper, sparkling in the sunlight, unable to touch him.

22

Libby's friend, Jessica Bay, was on Nantucket for only the day on business, but she wanted to speak to Lin as she walked to the docks to get the ferry so Lin met her at Libby's house and they strolled into town together. Jessica, in her mid-sixties, with short blond hair and bright blue eyes, was slim and medium height. She also had some paranormal skills and had a few experiences with ghosts.

"It's nice to meet you." With a warm smile, Jessica shook Lin's hand and then bent to pat Nicky who was practically smiling at the woman. "What an adorable dog." The comment made Nicky's tail wag even faster.

"Libby has told me a lot about you. Thanks for joining me as I head down to the ferry. The day has been so busy. I had several meetings and they all ran over and I need to be back on the mainland by this evening so I don't have the time I wanted to give you."

"I'm glad you asked me to walk into town with you." Lin told the woman about Ezra and Abigail Cooper and how they couldn't seem to find each other on the spirit plane. She explained Abigail's accidental death and Ezra's burden of grief that eventually did him in. "Someone new has inherited the Coopers' former home and has recently moved in. He feels overwhelmed by the sense of sadness that lingers in the house."

"He must be a sensitive man to be able to feel the emotions in the home." Jessica pulled her wheeled suitcase along the sidewalk behind her. "Ezra's grief was strong for wisps of it to still remain in the house."

"Do you have any idea why the ghosts aren't able to find each other?" Lin asked.

"There are some theories about why this sometimes happens, but I'm not sure I agree with any of them." Jessica's rolling suitcase got stuck on a loose sidewalk brick and she stopped to work it loose. "Some people think that spirits can't communicate with one another once they pass. That's nonsense. I know of a mother and daughter who were murdered and were separated for some time in the after-life. However, after an earthly year passed, they were reunited. They must have been able to communicate if they found each other so I don't agree that ghosts can't communicate together."

"What other theories are there?" Lin asked, intrigued by the topic.

"Some believe that spirits who have unfinished business on earth wander in the *in-between* ... not fully present on earth, yet do not cross over."

"How do the ghosts come to terms with their unfinished business?"

Jessica smiled at Lin. "By reaching out to people like you who can see them. Other spirits, unfortunately, never come to terms and continue to wander."

"Do you think that's happening with Ezra and Abigail?" Lin asked.

"It's possible. They're unable to connect, but probably yearn to do so. I'm sorry, but I don't know how you can help them in their search."

Lin's face looked crestfallen. "It's a puzzle. Maybe living people really can't help at all."

"I'm not sure that's the case. If there was nothing you could do, I don't think the ghosts would be trying to communicate with you," Jessica said.

"So maybe I *can* help?"

"I'd keep at it. We don't know that much about ghosts and the spirit-world. There's no reason not to be hopeful. How are the ghosts communicating with you?"

Lin told Jessica about the table tapping, how sometimes Sebastian, her ancestor, spoke a few words to her mind, yet mostly there was no direct communication and that she relied on the fact that sometimes where and when the ghosts appeared to her revealed clues to what they needed.

"This is all very interesting," Jessica said with a nod. "Your skills seem to be advancing at a brisk rate. As the years pass, you'll become a very important conduit for ghosts who need assistance."

Lin was surprised to hear this and deep-down wasn't sure it would ever be true.

As they approached the ferry, one attendant took Jessica's suitcase and a second attendant checked the ticket on her phone and gestured for her to head to the ramp for boarding.

Before they said goodbye, Lin asked for advice. "Do you have any thoughts about what I can do to help Ezra and Abigail?"

Jessica adjusted her carryon bag on her shoulder. "What I tell you will seem like nothing, but trust in your abilities. Spirits can take many forms. What seems like a problem can be a way to push someone to act in a way that solves an issue or brings the matter to a close. What's going on right now may seem like no progress is being made when in fact, it is a step toward the desired conclusion." The woman gave Lin a hug. "I hope next time, we can chat longer and that you'll be able to tell me that Ezra and Abigail have come together and their story has a happy ending."

Lin nodded and thanked Jessica and was sorry to see her go. She looked forward to meeting the woman again and engaging in a long conversation.

When she waved goodbye, Lin realized that she felt more hopeful and was grateful for the short time she had to talk things over with Jessica.

Walking back from the docks, she decided to window-shop in town for a little while before meeting Viv at her store in an hour. She stopped to admire some summer dresses on display in a small boutique's window and when she turned to continue her stroll, she almost bumped into Lori coming out of the store with a bag.

"Hi." Lori looked happy to see Lin. "I've been

shopping for a little while. I don't need anything, but I found a nice dress and decided to treat myself."

Lori didn't appear as upbeat as usual. "Is everything going okay?" Lin questioned.

"Yeah." Lori glanced around. "Well ... do you have a few minutes to sit?"

"Sure." Lin's heart began to pound with worry over what might be bothering Lori.

The two young women walked to a bench overlooking the harbor and sat together.

"I know every time I see you I talk about this, but you're the only one who doesn't look at me like I'm nuts." Lori let out a sigh and looked down at her hands.

"Have you been dreaming?" Lin asked.

"Yes." The word came out like a moan. "That dream is becoming more insistent. I'm not getting much sleep. I'm happy and peaceful when I'm in my *dream* house, but when I wake up, I feel agitated and anxious, and almost desperate. Like I *need* to find it. That I'm running out of time."

Lin's heart jumped into her throat in reaction to the urgency of Lori's feelings. *Why does she feel this way? What does it mean?*

"Heather asked me why I seem so tired. I couldn't tell her the reason. She thinks my dreams are nonsense and she's probably right." Lori sadly shook her head. "I made an appointment with a doctor to talk about my sleep problems. Maybe I can get hypnosis or something to help me let go of this dream."

"Do you want to let go of it?" Lin asked.

Lori lifted her eyes to Lin's and didn't answer for a few moments. "No. I don't." Letting out a sigh, she asked, "Why am I so obsessed with it? Why can't I dream about something else?"

"Do you ever dream about anything else?"

"Oh, sure, but the house dream always comes back with a vengeance."

"You'd probably miss it if it went away," Lin pointed out.

"I'd definitely miss it." Lori gave a half-smile. "I *would* like to get some sleep though."

"Tomorrow I'm going to look at a house with a friend of mine. You met him on the bike ride we all took together. John Clayton."

"The Realtor, right? He's marrying your cousin," Lori said.

"Right. The man who owns the house is considering selling it. John's going back to take some room measurements and to see it in daylight. The last time he went to do a walk-through, it was dark out. The house was built in the 1700s. It's a huge, beautiful Colonial near upper Main Street. Why don't you meet us there? You love the antique houses on-island. Walk around in it with me."

Lori's face brightened. "I'd love to see it. Are you thinking of buying it?"

With her eyes wide, Lin replied, "Oh, gosh, no. It's way too expensive for me. Maybe I'll be able to afford it in another life," she joked. "John knows I appreciate the old houses so he invited me to join him. I know the owner. Leonard and I do the landscaping there. We can tour the house and then I can show you the garden work we're doing."

"I'd love to see it." Lori asked where and when to meet.

"Invite Heather to join us. She might enjoy seeing the house, too," Lin said.

"I will." Lori's upbeat, positive nature seemed to be back to normal. "I'm excited about it. I'm really looking forward to it."

Some of the things Jessica had said to Lin as they walked to the ferry together kept drifting around in her head.

A problem can be a way to push someone to act in a way that solves an issue.

A step toward the desired conclusion.

What else did she say?

"Thanks for inviting me," Lori said. "I'll see you in the morning."

Lin shook herself from her thoughts. "You're very welcome. See you bright and early."

23

On her walk to Tim's house, Lin received a text from him that made her stop in her tracks.

I won't be at the house when you and John are there. I'm taking the ferry to the mainland. I'm going to stay in Boston indefinitely. I'll decide in a couple of weeks whether or not to sell the house. I'm leaning towards putting it on the market. Thanks for being a friend.

Lin's heart dropped. There was no way to keep Tim on the island without sounding crazy. *The ghost of my ancestor wants you to stay.*

With a heavy feeling of sadness, she continued on to Tim's Colonial and when she turned the corner, she saw John's car parked in the driveway and Lori coming up the sidewalk from the other direction.

"Heather couldn't come. I can't wait to see the house. Is that it?" Lori's eyes scanned the front of the yellow Colonial with the daffodils growing in the front. "What a beauty."

"The owner had to go to the mainland so he won't be here to show us around," Lin told her. "John's inside already. Why don't we go in?"

The front door was unlocked and the women stepped into the foyer.

"John?" Lin called. "We're here."

John spoke from the kitchen. "I'm in back."

Lin turned towards Lori to ask if she wanted to wander through the house together while John was busy.

Lori's eyes sparkled as she took in the carved wooden staircase, the tall ceilings, the chandelier. She ran her hand over the wood of the bannister like it was made of gold. She stepped into the sitting room on the right and walked around staring at everything ... the fireplace, the furniture, the huge windows.

Lin stood at the threshold watching her friend, the young woman's face lit up, her eyes sparkling. All of a sudden, Lori raced from the room to the sitting parlor off the foyer and stood at the entrance taking everything in, then she hurried to the library and then to the dining room. When she reached the kitchen, she turned all around. "This is an addition."

Lin followed Lori's every step through the downstairs rooms without saying anything.

Lori was practically running through the house. She returned to the foyer and tore up the staircase to the second floor hurrying through the rooms.

"Do you like the house?" Lin asked, not understanding why the little blond hairs on her arms were standing up.

Lori made eye contact with Lin, her eyes welling up. She didn't answer the question, but hurried down the hall to the room Tim was using as an office.

When the two young women entered the room, Lin's skin felt like it was being pricked with tiny needles.

Lori took hold of Lin's arm and when she spoke, her voice was heavy and hoarse. "I know this house."

"You've been here before?" Lin asked, her head feeling dizzy.

With a nod, Lori moved slowly around the room. "I know every inch of this house. Not the kitchen or the solarium, those are additions. This is the first time I've seen them, but I know everything else. Some of the furniture is the same, too. I could find my way around in here with my eyes closed."

Lin's stomach tightened. "Is this...?"

"This is the house in my dreams." Lori practically whispered. She batted at the tears that were rolling down her cheeks. "I found it. I found it. I can't believe I found it." She stared at Lin, her cheeks pink with excitement. "Who lives here?"

"Tim Pierce. He's an architect. He inherited the house from his grandfather. The grandfather lived here for many years."

"Tim Pierce? How old is he? Is he old?"

"He's about thirty," Lin told her.

Lori walked around the room lovingly touching the walls and the woodwork. "How do I know this house?"

"You think you've been in here before?"

Lori gave a quick nod. "But how could I have been? I don't remember being brought here when I was little. I guess I could have though. Was Tim Pierce's grandfather's last name Pierce, too?"

"It was," Lin said.

"I don't remember that name. I don't remember my parents talking about anyone with that name. But I know this house like the back of my hand."

Lori stood before a built-in bookcase and gently rested her palm against the fine wood. "This isn't really a book shelf. Do you know that?"

A shiver ran down Lin's back. "What is it?" Some of the words Jessica had said to her the other day about problems and ghosts rang in her head, but none of it seemed to be of help.

Lori moved to one end of the bookcase and pushed on it. To Lin's amazement, the shelves moved and slid seamlessly over the floor.

"It's really a door," Lori said. "See?"

Lin could see the little railing of an interior balcony appear behind where the bookcase had been. She stepped forward and looked down into a family room, an addition to the main house.

"This was added, too, but it was here when I was here before." Lori took a deep breath and gingerly took a few steps to the balcony to stand beside Lin ... and then she let out a little gasp. "In my dream, there's a rocking chair in that room over there by the window."

"I remember you told me that," Lin said.

"I...." Lori's hands trembled as she held onto the railing with both of her hands. Tears of joy began to fall from her eyes, and she bowed her head slightly.

"What? What is it?" Lin asked.

"In...." Lori couldn't get the words out. Putting a hand on her chest, she tried again. "In my dream, there's always a woman sitting in the rocker. She looks out the window. She's wearing a blue dress, the kind of dress that someone from the late 1700s would wear. She's in her mid-twenties. Part of her hair is up in a little twist at the back of her head." Lori's chest was rapidly rising and falling. "The rest of her hair falls around her shoulders. I never see her face in my dreams." The young woman turned a little to face Lin. "But I ... I know who she is. Now I know who she is."

Lin's head tilted to the side. "Who is she?" she asked softly.

Lori took Lin's hands in hers. Her voice shook when she said, "The woman in the rocker by the window ... that woman ... is *me*."

Lin felt like she'd been hit by a ton of bricks. Her head spun and her knees went weak. "How can that be?"

"I have no idea." Lori put her hands over her face. "I don't know how it's possible, but I know for sure ... I *am* the woman in that rocking chair."

Jessica's voice played in Lin's head. *Ghosts can take many forms.*

Lin stared into Lori's face. "Abigail?" The word floated like a wisp of air.

For a second, Lori's eyes almost showed recognition, but then confusion washed over her expression. "Who?"

Adrenaline raced through Lin's veins. "Is the name Ezra familiar to you? Ezra Cooper?"

Lori blinked several times. "I ... don't know. Is he someone I know?"

"My head is spinning," Lin stepped back from the balcony and sat down on a small sofa.

"I'm not crazy," Lori told her.

"Oh, I know that." Lin closed her eyes for a moment, her hand reaching for her horseshoe necklace. *What's going on? Is Lori Abigail? Is this Lori's second chance at life? I mean ... is this Abigail's second chance at life?*

Lin opened her eyes and stood up. "I believe you. How do you feel? Is all of this frightening to you?"

The tiniest of smiles turned up the corners of Lori's lips. "I've never felt so calm, so peaceful. I don't know what's going on, but it doesn't scare me at all. I feel so ... centered. I feel like I know the answer to a question I never knew existed." The young woman's eyes welled up. "Lin. Have I lived before? That's it, isn't it?"

All the pieces of the crazy puzzle began to swirl in Lin's head until they settled and lined up and fell into place. "I don't understand it, but it is what it is." She pulled out her phone and sent a text to Tim hoping the ferry hadn't yet left.

Don't leave. I have to tell you something. I'm coming to the dock. Please don't leave.

"I have to go, but I won't be gone long. I'll be back in a few minutes. Come downstairs and wait for me, okay? Will you stay here with John until I come back?"

Lori smiled. "I don't ever want to leave this house."

"Hurry downstairs with me. I have to go." Lin jogged out of the room and down to the first floor where she nearly ran into John in the hall. "I have to go somewhere. Stay here, will you? Lori's going to stay, too. Please stay here."

John gave Lin a look. "Are you okay?"

"I'll explain everything when I get back." Lin rushed for the front door, bolted outside and down the walkway to the sidewalk, and then she ran like she'd never run before.

She heard the ferry's horn let out a long, slow blast.

Please don't be on that ferry.

Dashing down Main Street, Lin heard a man call her name, and when she saw who it was, she stopped so fast, she lost her footing and almost fell forward.

24

"Tim." Lin leaned over to catch her breath. "I was worried you wouldn't get my text before you boarded the ferry."

"You sent me a text?" The young man reached into his briefcase and removed his phone. When he read the message, he looked keenly at Lin. "Is there an emergency? Is that why you were running to the dock?"

From the revelation at the house and the run down the streets, Lin was still trying to catch her breath and slow her heart rate. "No. Yes. I mean there's nothing wrong with your house, but...." She let her voice trail off.

"But what? Is something wrong? Has something

happened?" Trying to figure out what the problem was, Tim's eyes stared into Lin's.

"There's nothing wrong." Lin noticed the man's rolling suitcase. "If you didn't get my text, why aren't you on the ferry?"

Tim exhaled. "I decided not to go. I decided to come home for a while and think things through. It felt wrong to leave. Who knows why?" He shook his head in confusion. "I was standing in line on the dock waiting to board. I was sure I was making the right decision to return to Boston. Then something came over me ... I can't describe it. I know it sounds ridiculous, but I knew I had to come back to the house."

"You felt you were making the wrong decision to leave?"

"Yeah." Tim face suddenly looked washed in doubt. "Maybe I don't know what I'm doing. Maybe I feel guilty about selling the house and I had a momentary lapse in judgment and decided to come back." Letting out a sigh, he asked, "Why am I so messed up? I've never been so indecisive and uncertain."

"How do you feel right now, standing here with me? There's another ferry in an hour. If I told you that you had to decide in two seconds, what would your choice be?"

"Um."

"Give me your answer without thinking about it," Lin urged. "What pops into your mind?"

"I'd stay."

"Do you know there's a secret bookcase in your office that slides away to reveal a Juliet-balcony looking down into the family room?"

Tim's eyes widened. "John found it, did he?"

"I found it," Lin said. "Actually, someone else found it, but I was there when the bookcase was pushed back. Did your grandfather add that feature?"

"No, it was there when he bought the house. I thought it was cool." A smile lifted the young man's face. "When I was a kid, I pretended it was a secret spy entrance. Sometimes, I pretended I was giving a speech to my forces below in the family room." Tim chuckled at the memory.

"The house holds some nice memories for you," Lin smiled, hoping there would be even better memories created for Tim in that house in the coming years.

"So what was so urgent that I wasn't supposed to get on the ferry?" Tim asked.

"Why don't I show you?" Lin turned and they walked up the sidewalk towards the house.

The closer they got to the Colonial, the more nervous Lin became and the faster her heart began to beat.

As they rounded the corner, they saw John standing on the sidewalk photographing the front of the antique home from different angles. When he spotted them approaching, he waved and waited for them to come up to him. "I thought you were heading back to Boston?" John said to Tim.

Tim looked from John to Lin, confused about why John didn't know Lin asked him to return to the house.

"Why did you want him to come back?" John tilted his head in question.

"I'll tell you later." Lin nudged Tim's arm to indicate they should go inside.

"I'm going to take some more pictures of the house," John told them as they walked away. "Lori's in the kitchen."

"Who's Lori?" Tim asked.

"She's a lawyer. She's related to Leonard's girlfriend. She just moved to the island and she loves old houses. I hope it's okay that I invited her to come in and see your home while John was doing the measurements."

"Sure. It's fine." Tim lifted his suitcase through the front door and wheeled it into the foyer just as Lori came down the hall.

"You're back," Lori said to Lin and then she stopped short when she saw Tim in the entryway.

Tim looked at the young woman just as Lin introduced them.

"This is Lori Michaels. This is Tim Pierce, the owner of the house." Lin watched them to see how they would regard one another.

Neither of the young people said a word for several long moments, they only stood staring at each other.

Lin could see Lori's eyes fill up with tears as she stood looking at the good-looking man across from her. She could also see that Tim appeared to be choked up.

And then the cold enveloped her and when she turned her head towards Lori, Abigail Cooper was standing right behind her, shimmering and glowing. The ghost's eyes were staring straight ahead over Lori's shoulder.

When Lin looked to see what Abigail was transfixed by, she saw Ezra Cooper standing close behind

Tim, his atoms translucent and glittering, his sparkling eyes pinned onto Abigail.

Lin was so stunned to see the four people together in the foyer, that she was unable to speak.

"Have we met before?" Tim took a few steps closer to the sandy-haired, blue-eyed woman. "I feel like I know you."

Lori smiled, blinked her tears away, and cleared her throat. "I'm not sure. We might have."

"On second thought, we couldn't have met before, because I would never have forgotten you." Tim reached out to shake hands with Lori and when their hands touched, they both felt a little spark jump between their skin.

Lori chuckled, her cheeks tinging pink. "It must be static electricity."

The two young people shifted around on their feet a bit, grinning and acting slightly self-conscious, clearly very attracted to one another.

"Can I get you something to drink?" Tim realized he was still holding Lori's hand and he sheepishly let it go.

Ezra and Abigail floated over the floor towards each other with outstretched hands, their eyes full of love, each one shining in silver and gold. When their fingers touched, a flash of light shot up to the ceiling, but only Lin could see the ghosts and what was happening.

The atoms of the two spirits seemed to blend together and swirl gently in the air, before returning to their own separate forms. The ghosts turned to look at Lin. Hand in hand, Ezra and Abigail met Lin's eyes. Their hands covered their hearts in thanks, and then their atoms flashed so brightly that Lin had to close her eyes for a moment, and when she opened them, the ghosts were gone.

"Lin, would you like to have a drink with us? Coffee? Tea? Do you think John would like something?" Tim asked.

Lori had moved closer to the young man, their shoulders almost touching, and they kept glancing at one another with beaming smiles.

"I'll go ask him," Lin nodded.

"Did Lin show you the whole house?" Tim asked Lori. "I'd be glad to give you a tour."

Lori gave Lin a knowing look. They both were aware that she was familiar with every inch of the Colonial.

"I'd love to have a tour." Lori nodded at Tim.

Lin said, "I'll go get John and see if he's done. We'll meet you in the kitchen."

Her heart full to bursting, Lin found John in the yard.

"What's up with you?" John asked. "You look like you've never been happier."

"Maybe I haven't." Lin grinned.

"Why did Tim come back?"

Lin took in a long breath. "Fate told him to."

John raised an eyebrow. "What's going on?"

Lin swallowed to clear the emotion from her voice. "Two ghosts just found each other."

John made a face as he shook his head and laughed. "Those two people in the house are flesh and blood. They're not ghosts."

Lin looked to the front door. "No, they're not, but I think they used to be. Lori knows this house. She used to live here ... in another life. And now she and Tim have found each other and are getting a second chance at life ... together."

25

When John heard what Lin told him about two spirits who had found each other and were getting a second chance to live a life together, he almost dropped to the grass in a faint. He didn't want to join Tim and Lori for a cold drink so he and Lin made excuses and left the Colonial which was just as well. Lin thought the couple should spend the time together.

Lin, Jeff, Viv, and John spent the day on the water on John's boat. It was a warm spring day with a beautiful blue sky dotted with a few high, puffy clouds. The foursome, and Nicky and Queenie enjoyed the afternoon boat ride around the island and being out in Nantucket Sound between the island and the mainland.

Returning to the dock, they prepared dinner and enjoyed drinks with crackers and cheese sitting on the boat as the sun set in the distance.

While waiting for the macaroni and cheese to bake in the boat's galley, salads were served, and the dog and cat were fed. After eating, Nicky and Queenie curled up on the deck and had a snooze.

"I still don't get it." John poured sparkling water into everyone's glasses. "How can Lori and Tim be Abigail and Ezra? It makes no sense at all."

"It makes *perfect* sense." Viv lifted a forkful of the salad. "Ezra and Abigail's spirits wandered around searching for each other. We think Lori and Tim are Abigail and Ezra's spirits living today."

John still looked dumbfounded.

"When a friend of Libby's met with me a few days ago," Lin said, "she told me ghosts can take different forms. We didn't have time to discuss it further because she needed to get to the ferry. Libby has always told me that we can't hope to understand the spirit world. We can only work with what we experience when interacting with ghosts and help them as best we can."

"I don't think going over it and going over it in our heads will help either," Jeff said. "It's impossible for us to understand, but we can be happy for Ezra and Abigail for having a second chance at life together. We have to accept that we can't make sense of any of it. It just ... is." Jeff shrugged.

Lin added, "Ezra and Abigail wanted me to help them find each other. My mistake was that I thought they wanted to reunite in the spirit world. What they really wanted was for Lori and Tim to find each other so they could reunite in *today's* world. As long as I brought them together, I fulfilled my part in all of it."

John let out a groan. "It all sounds perfectly reasonable when you're telling me these things. It's when my brain tries to understand how two spirits can be four different people is where I start to have a nervous breakdown."

The people listening to John couldn't help but laugh.

"My advice is to stop thinking about it," Jeff said with a smile, "and just accept there are things that happen that we can't fathom."

"Okay." John sipped from his bottle of beer. "I'm going to pretend that Lin and Viv are normal people, that there are ghosts that buzz around, but I don't have to understand any part of it."

"Excellent," Viv told her fiancé.

"Except the ghosts don't *buzz* around and Viv and I *are* normal people," Lin protested.

John rolled his eyes. "Define *normal*."

Lin ignored the comment and changed the subject. "Lori and Tim have seen each other every day for the past two weeks. They're over the moon with each other."

"Do they know they lived before in the 1700s?" John asked.

Lin said, "Lori knows she lived in the Colonial a very long time ago. She knew every inch of that house when I first brought her there. Lori told me the second she laid eyes on Tim, she knew they'd had a relationship in the past and would be important to one another in the present. She doesn't need to know all the details. She only needs to know they're happy together."

Viv nodded. "Lori told me she felt like she'd been searching for Tim and had finally found him. Tim feels that Lori is the one he's been longing for. He's staying on-island. He told us he isn't lonely or anxious anymore. He's found what he's always needed."

"It's really quite a love story," Jeff said and took Lin's hand in his.

"Only no one would ever believe certain parts of

it." With an involuntary shiver, John went down to the galley to take the macaroni and cheese out of the oven. Viv went along to bring up a pan of roasted tomatoes, onions, and mushrooms sprinkled with feta cheese.

Candles were lit on the table and the group settled around to enjoy the food.

"What do we all think of Tim's offer to have our wedding ceremony in his backyard?" Jeff passed the platter of roasted vegetables to Viv.

"I love the idea," Viv said.

"Me, too," Lin nodded. "After Leonard and I finish the landscaping, it's going to be really beautiful."

John said warily, "As long as no ghosts come to the ceremony, it's fine with me."

"Tim is very generous to offer the yard to us," Jeff said. "He's going to provide drinks and hors d'oeuvres with butler service for all the guests prior to the ceremony."

John smiled. "Tim said it's the least he can do since he decided not to sell the Colonial and deprived me out of the hefty commission."

"What if it rains that day?" Jeff questioned. "It's New England. It could be ninety degrees and humid, or pouring rain and cold."

"Tim is going to watch the weather," Lin said. "If it's going to be too hot or too rainy, he'll have a tent set up either with portable air conditioning or heaters."

"That guy thinks of everything," John said, and then kiddingly added, "but he *has* lived more than one lifetime so he's had lots of experience with the weather."

Viv gave John a playful bop on the arm. "Who knows? Maybe you've lived before, too."

John's face drained of color. "No way. Once is enough for me."

"I just remembered something Lori used to say about her dream," Jeff said. "She told you the woman who sat in the rocking chair in the Colonial was always looking out the window at the water. But there's no view of water from the house."

"Lori looked that up at the historical museum," Lin said. "In the 1700s, there was a small pond at the rear of the property that dried up over time and was filled in with soil. She was sure the woman in the rocker, who was actually her, was gazing out at water so she had to find out about it."

"Does Lori remember being Abigail?" Viv asked.

"Only tiny bits and pieces. She knows the Colonial and she recognizes Tim from long ago, and now has snippets of memories of sitting in the rocking chair. She doesn't recall the fall that took Abigail's life. Once in a while, something bubbles up that seems familiar, but she can't remember much about it."

Jeff said, "It sounds like that déjà vu feeling we all have on occasion."

After the meal, the foursome decided to walk the few blocks into town to get some ice cream cones. Nicky and Queenie chose to stay on the boat and watch the people strolling by.

Even though it was still spring, the streets were busy with tourists, sightseers, and townspeople walking past stores, heading to restaurants, going down to the docks, and meeting friends.

"It's going to be a busy summer," Viv pointed out. "The island gets crowded earlier and earlier."

"I love the bustle. I love the good weather." Lin held Jeff's hand. "I love it when it's time for the tourists to flock here."

After getting cones, they walked around town and then headed back to the docks.

Under the streetlamps, Lin and Jeff stood by the water with their arms around each other's waists watching a ferry from the mainland slide into its berth.

"We're pretty lucky, aren't we?" Lin asked. "We live in this beautiful place. We love our jobs. We have good friends. We have each other."

Jeff kissed her on the top of her head. "I knew I was lucky the day I found you."

A cold breeze blew over Lin and out of the corner of her eye, she saw two ghosts shimmering under the lamplight.

Sebastian and Emily.

They held Lin's eyes and nodded to her.

And then she heard words form inside her head.

Thank you for your help.

Lin placed her hand over her heart and smiled at the spirits.

The ghosts held hands while their atoms swirled and glowed, and then in a white flash of light, they were gone.

Lin thought about how, in the past, she wanted nothing to do with her skill. She wanted it to go away and never come back. But now, she loved her ability to see and interact with ghosts and she wouldn't want to be anywhere else, doing anything else, with anyone else other than the people she loved on this island.

She looked up at Jeff and whispered something into his ear, and then he smiled, leaned down and gently kissed his fiancée as they stood together by the glistening ocean lit up by a million, sparkling stars.

I hope you enjoyed *The Haunted Past*! The next book in the series, *The Haunted Wedding*, can be found here:

viewbook.at/TheHauntedWedding

THANK YOU FOR READING!

Books by J.A. WHITING can be found here:
www.amazon.com/author/jawhiting

To hear about new books and book sales, please sign up for our mailing list at:
www.jawhiting.com

Your email will never be sold, shared, or spammed.

If you enjoyed the book, please consider leaving a review. A few words are all that's needed. It would be very much appreciated.

BOOKS BY J. A. WHITING

SWEET COVE PARANORMAL COZY MYSTERIES

LIN COFFIN PARANORMAL COZY MYSTERIES

CLAIRE ROLLINS PARANORMAL COZY MYSTERIES

MURDER POSSE PARANORMAL COZY MYSTERIES

PAXTON PARK PARANORMAL COZY MYSTERIES

ELLA DANIELS WITCH COZY MYSTERIES

SEEING COLORS PARANORMAL COZY MYSTERIES

OLIVIA MILLER MYSTERIES (not cozy)

SWEET ROMANCES by JENA WINTER

COZY BOX SETS

BOOKS BY J.A. WHITING & NELL MCCARTHY

HOPE HERRING PARANORMAL COZY MYSTERIES

TIPPERARY CARRIAGE COMPANY COZY MYSTERIES

BOOKS BY J.A. WHITING & ARIEL SLICK

GOOD HARBOR WITCHES PARANORMAL COZY MYSTERIES

BOOKS BY J.A. WHITING & AMANDA DIAMOND

PEACHTREE POINT COZY MYSTERIES

DIGGING UP SECRETS PARANORMAL COZY MYSTERIES

BOOKS BY J.A. WHITING & MAY STENMARK

MAGICAL SLEUTH PARANORMAL WOMEN'S FICTION COZY MYSTERIES

HALF MOON PARANORMAL MYSTERIES

VISIT US

www.jawhiting.com

www.bookbub.com/authors/j-a-whiting

www.amazon.com/author/jawhiting

www.facebook.com/jawhitingauthor

www.bingebooks.com/author/ja-whiting

J. A. WHITING BOOKS

Printed in Great Britain
by Amazon